THE ARRANGEMENT

DELANEY DIAMOND

GARDEN AVENUE PRESS

The Arrangement by Delaney Diamond

To Monique and Ana for believing in me.

CHAPTER 1

"I'll do it, but there are conditions," Leonardo da Silva said.

His name meant "strong as a lion," and he was aptly named. He had the strength and cunning of the large cat, and he never hesitated to tear apart his rivals in business. His ruthlessness was not a personality trait that made him well-liked in the business world. It made him a worthy adversary, feared more than respected.

Alexa da Silva held her breath as she stared at the broad, muscular back of her soon-to-be ex-husband. Her eyes were drawn lower to his butt, shown to advantage because he'd chosen to shove his hands into his pockets, which stretched the tailored trousers taut against his firm posterior.

She lifted her gaze, reminding herself why she was there. She had just asked him to help her brother, Xander, out of a financial debacle. She'd known there would be a catch, of course, but what exactly he would demand in return remained to be revealed.

It had taken every ounce of courage she'd had to walk

through the doors of the high-rise building he owned in Atlanta and ask for this favor, buoyed by her brother's pleading request.

* * *

"LEXIE, please, you've got to ask him. Leo is the only person I know who has enough money to get me out of this."

"I haven't seen Leo in months," she'd explained to her brother. "It's only a matter of time before he files for divorce. I'm surprised he hasn't done it already."

"All the more reason to ask him now, before he does it," Xander had offered helpfully. As if it were as simple as merely asking for Leo's help.

Sighing, Alexa had shaken her head. "I don't know if I can do that, Xander. I left him, and now you want me to go back and ask him for money? He's not going to just hand it over to me. There's just got to be another alternative."

* * *

BUT THERE HADN'T BEEN, despite leaving no stone unturned. No one else they knew had the kind of money Xander needed, and given the financial straits he was in, getting another loan was impossible.

Now here she was, sitting across from the modern, mini-malist glass desk and the floor-to-ceiling windows Leonardo was staring out of, hoping he wouldn't laugh her out of the office because she had the audacity, after all this time, to come ask him for money. This was a low point in her life, but she and Xander were close, and she would do anything for him.

With trepidation, Alexa asked, "What are your conditions?"

She stiffened her spine, ready to negotiate on whatever point her husband would bring up. Even as she thought about it, she almost laughed at the idea that she could negotiate on the same level as him. Leonardo was a shrewd businessman, having expanded his family's multimillion-dollar telecommunications enterprise into a multi-country empire that worked on projects across the United States and Europe.

He turned, as if suddenly remembering she was in the office. Alexa braced herself. When he faced her, she noted how the angular lines of his face looked harsher, more pronounced than they were before their separation. Still, he was handsome, despite the hardened square jaw and unwelcoming charcoal eyes.

Half Brazilian, he had his mother's dark coloring and spoke with a slight accent because he'd spent thirteen years of his life in Brazil after his parents divorced when he was five. His wavy dark brown hair, which he tended to wear a little too long, curled along the collar of his shirt. He was a big man, with a powerful chest and large, muscular arms.

His mother had married the eldest son of a wealthy Georgia family who owned the number one telecommunications company in the South. Proud of her heritage, she had insisted he should be born in Brazil. After the divorce, she returned to Brazil with him. She resorted back to her maiden name and changed Leonardo's as well. It had been a crushing blow to his father. Leonardo returned to the States at the age of eighteen to go to school and work at his father's firm. As was expected, when Leonardo's father retired, the reins of the company were turned over to him. At thirty-three years old, he was already a seasoned professional. He'd taken Radiant Communications from a regional powerhouse and transformed it into one of the largest firms in the industry.

"First, he has to agree to hire an office manager to help him manage his bills and payments."

Alexa nodded in agreement. No argument there. It was something she herself had told Xander on more than one occasion he needed to do, but he was the stubborn, creative type, more concerned with the culinary arts than managing the business side of things. That explained how he'd gotten into this dire situation.

"Second, I want you to come home and resume our marriage."

Alexa's eyes widened. It was amazing how he managed to state so calmly a sentence that obliterated every ounce of oxygen from the room and shattered what little peace of mind she had left.

She laughed, stunned. "What did you say?" She must not have heard him correctly.

"You heard me," Leonardo replied, his face betraying no emotion. He walked over to the desk, in front of which she sat, and braced one hip against the edge, crossing his powerful arms and looking down his hawklike nose at her.

Alexa shook her head, nervously running her fingers through her short black curls in a futile attempt to calm the erratic beating of her heart. His unexpected request rattled her more than she wanted to betray. She took a calming breath.

"You're being absurd, Leo," she said, looking up at him. From her seated position, he looked formidable. "I wouldn't move back into the mansion if you were the last man on . . ." Alexa let her voice trail off when she realized what she had been about to say. She forced herself to calm down and think of Xander. She couldn't screw this up. He was depending on her.

Leonardo lifted one thick eyebrow in mock inquiry. "If I were the last man on earth who could get Xander out of the mess he's in?"

Alexa pressed her lips together before answering, taking time to formulate her words carefully. "We're getting a divorce."

"Are we? Did I miss something? I was never served with divorce papers. Should I contact my attorney to find out if he's forgotten to send me the documents?" His tone was mocking.

"You're going to divorce me."

She was certain of it. It was only a matter of time. She had embarrassed Leonardo by leaving him, and there was no doubt in her mind he would eventually eradicate her from his life completely. That's how he operated. When he was done, there would be no trace of her left in his life.

"I'm not the one who walked out," he said pointedly. "You did. I never wanted our marriage to end. Have you forgotten?"

Alexa took a deep breath and got to her feet. "I haven't forgotten, and you know why I left." She threw all caution to the wind. "It's not as if you paid me any attention when I was there. You never acted like a man who was married. Between the long hours at work and the women falling all over you everywhere we went, I'm surprised you even noticed I was gone."

A muscle in his jaw tensed. "Oh, I noticed."

He spoke quietly, but Alexa heard the menacing undertone as loudly as a drumbeat. She knew she had grated on a still raw nerve.

Alexa took another deep breath. "Leo, this is ridiculous. I'm not moving back in with you."

She turned around, about to snatch up her purse from the chair, when he said, "So what are you going to tell your brother?" His voice was still quiet.

Gritting her teeth, she flashed him her most withering gaze. "You've reached a new low," she bit out.

Leonardo smiled, completely unmoved by her disparaging remark. He had the upper hand.

"There's the fire that I'm used to," he murmured. "That little helpless act you came in here with was not very convincing."

"It wasn't an act," Alexa said, standing tall. "But it seems you prefer for me to come out fighting. I would have thought you'd want me begging for your mercy—groveling, on my hands and knees."

He tilted his head, as if contemplating what she said. "Hmm .

. . just on your knees . . . doing those amazing things you do with your . . . mouth."

Alexa inhaled sharply, shocked at the suggestion and the images it conjured. Her heart rate picked up as she recalled a time when she had done just that in this very office, unselfishly offering pleasure to the husband she adored. The honeymoon period didn't last long, though. About one month, to be exact, before business took precedence in his life and her own self-doubt exacerbated the tension between them.

"That was out of line."

"No, it wasn't, *querida*." He smiled, the devastating smile she found irresistible. "You're my wife, and you do have an amazing mouth."

Alexa clenched her purse, ignoring the heart-wrenching familiarity of the Portuguese endearment and fighting back the sensuous images that were now emblazoned in her mind's eye. "Yes, I'm your wife, but we both know that's in name only. We haven't lived together as husband and wife for months."

"That's easily rectified by a mutually satisfying arrangement," Leonardo reminded her.

"What is it that you're suggesting? That we just pick up where we left off and act as if we're reconciled?"

"That's exactly what I'm suggesting. It would be perfect—like a business deal where both parties get what they want."

"You've ventured into a new business now? Buying and selling women?"

She saw the anger flash in his eyes before he could conceal it, and she gloated a little that she'd gotten under his skin.

"You should be careful what you say. Remember, you're the one who sought me out to ask for money." He brushed imaginary lint from his shirtsleeve. "Maybe we should forget the whole thing."

He turned away from her in a dismissive fashion, and she panicked.

"No, wait!"

Alexa grasped onto his arm as if it were a lifeline, feeling the heat of his muscles bunch against her palm. He looked down at her fingers, and she released him. He turned slowly, and she knew in that moment the tables turned. He knew how desperate she was, and he would use it to his advantage.

"Yes?" One dark brow lifted toward his hairline.

"I can at least hear you out," Alexa said. She couldn't believe what she was saying, even though the words fell from her own lips. "What would you . . . expect?"

"I would expect you to resume all your wifely duties, including sharing my bed." He didn't flinch.

She swallowed. "Think about what you're asking me to do." Alexa faced him full-on. "I'm not a prostitute."

"I agree. Once again, you're my wife. All I'm asking is that you behave like you are."

"Why are you doing this? It's been four months." Alexa was appalled by the near panic in her voice, but she was ill-prepared to conceal it. This was like something out of a nightmare, and she wanted no part of it, but Alexa knew if she didn't comply with his demand, he would allow her brother to be crushed. If she could just reason with him, then maybe they could agree to an alternative. "There must be another way—another answer."

"When you think of it, let me know," Leonardo said, just before he folded his arms across his chest again.

Standing before him, all of a sudden Alexa felt much smaller than her five feet five inches, despite wearing heels that added another four inches to her height. He was just that tall—and broad, too. She felt like an insignificant little pea.

The ball was back in her court, and they both knew she could offer nothing to bargain with. He was in an enviable position, with nothing to lose. She needed him, not the other way around.

"I shouldn't have come here," Alexa said, her voice laced with bitterness. "I should've known you wouldn't show me any mercy."

"I've shown you plenty of mercy," Leonardo said, placing his fingertips on the cool glass surface of the desk. He leaned toward Alexa. "I've allowed you to enter my office, when I could have refused to see you and asked my assistant to tell you to leave. Or better yet, I could have had security escort you from the building."

He looked her up and down, a withering appraisal that silently shredded the sleeveless ruffled top and flowing skirt.

"You want mercy after what you did? After you walked out on me and I didn't hear from you for months?" He laughed, but there was no humor in the sound. "Now you come back here, asking me for money. What would you do if you were me, Alexa?"

"If it makes you feel any better," he continued, "you'll only have to suffer through our marriage for two more months, and then I'll give you the divorce you've obviously been wanting but were afraid to ask for."

"Two months?" she repeated, frowning. "Why two months?"

"I have my reasons," he said in a clipped tone.

"What if we get tired of each other before that? What then?"

The grim set of his face betrayed no emotion. "We'll cross that bridge when we get to it."

For several moments, Alexa mulled the idea around in her head. "Two months?" she asked. "That's it—nothing more?"

"Unless you want more?"

"You wish." Alexa turned her back on him to think clearly.

Two months. Sixty days. Not an eternity, but it could seem like it if she moved back in with Leonardo and was subjected to whatever his demands were. There was no telling how many ways he had conjured up to punish her for what she did. She knew he would be merciless because she'd seen how he handled business opponents who crossed him.

"Come now, Alexa," he crooned, directly behind her now.

She could feel his warm breath fan across the nape of her neck. She shut her eyes briefly and wished she didn't enjoy it, wished she didn't want more than that featherlight sensation. She shouldn't. She needed his help, but he was still the enemy, and her body refused to acknowledge that. Instead, a tingling sensation crept along her inner thighs.

"Even if we were not compatible in other areas of our marriage, we never had problems satisfying each other in bed."

Alexa's pulse quickened at the intimate tone of his voice, the way it dropped several octaves and whispered across her skin like a caress.

"That's beside the point."

She swallowed past the lump that formed out of nowhere in her throat. She didn't want to admit how correct he was. They had always been great together. She had always found him irresistible, with his strong jaw, smooth, beautiful bronzed skin, and a perfect, muscular male body that could put any Greek god to shame.

"The choice is yours, Alexa. You came here for a reason, to get money for your brother. I'm willing to give you the money."

She whirled around, drawing a sharp breath at his close proximity. She made an impulsive step back.

"You'll do it, but for a price. There're strings attached."

"Did you think you could come here and charm me into handing over such a large sum of money—for nothing?"

She hadn't really thought that, but she'd hoped it was a possibility. She wouldn't admit it, though. It was ludicrous for her to even have considered coming here, much less asking for money. If she hadn't been so desperate to help her brother, she would have never needed to step foot in Leonardo's opulent office again. She decided to try one more time to reason with him.

"Are there any other terms you'd consider? We could pay you back, Leo. It would take time, but—"

"You couldn't afford the interest," he interrupted in a brusque tone. His chiseled face became as hard as stone. There was no softness in him at all toward her or her predicament. "Your brother's a high risk. Besides, that's not what I want. I told you what I want. Now you need to make a decision."

CHAPTER 2

"*I* know I do." Alexa clenched her fist. "Why don't we just call it what it really is? Revenge. Pure and simple. You want to take your revenge on me because I dared walk out on you, and no one walks out on Leonardo da Silva!"

She was talking too much, being reckless. This was not the way to convince Leonardo to help her. Yet she couldn't stop the rush of words. She and Xander had exhausted every possibility before she came here, and she wished she didn't have to ask him for anything.

His demeanor changed. Where he was cold before, he was now fuming, hot anger rolling off him in waves, a palpable entity that reached the few feet between them to warn her she was treading on dangerous ground.

His eyes narrowed to slits so thin all she could see was the glitter of his pupils as he looked down at her with ill-concealed anger.

"Don't flatter yourself into thinking that abandoning our marriage mattered more to me than it did."

The cutting words were an effective slap in the face, meant to put her in her place and remind her of how little she meant to him. She didn't need reminding, though. She recalled very well the nights she spent alone in their vast bed while he traveled or worked late. Or the nights he claimed to work late and came home exhausted, never touching her and falling asleep, only to awaken and leave again in the morning before she awoke.

She would never forget how other women clamored for his attention, as if she weren't in the room. Did he ever turn them away, or stop the behavior? No. Her presence did nothing to stop the women or him from their flirtations, and it hurt. It hurt more than she would like to admit right now.

"Then why ask me back, if I'm so unimportant? If it's not revenge, then what is it?" Fool that she was, she held her breath with the hope that his answer would contain a modicum of kindness. Of course it didn't.

"Because you need to be taught a lesson, and I'd like to think of myself as a good teacher. You see, there are consequences for one's actions, and to expect to walk in here and not have to do anything in return—well, that's simply ridiculous. I'm a businessman, and I would never agree to that kind of deal."

"I didn't expect to not have to do anything. As I told you, you would get your money back. I didn't think you would just give it to me and it wouldn't have to be repaid. Let's discuss the terms, and we can draw up a contract."

Leonardo shook his head. "How could you possibly afford my terms? Because of course, I would set the terms, not you." He tapped a finger on his desk. "Trust me, Alexa, I'm doing you a favor. You're learning a valuable lesson, and I'm getting a much better return on my investment than if I gave you the option of paying me back."

How he managed to convince himself he was doing her a favor was beyond her.

"There has to be another way."

"There is. Get your brother to dig himself out of the hole he's dug for himself."

He knew there was nowhere else for them to turn. She'd basically told him that, and her presence in his office was a clear indication they lacked other options. He had to know he was the last person she would ever seek assistance from if there were another avenue to pursue to resolve Xander's financial problem.

"There's nothing I can do to change your mind?"

"Nothing," he said with finality.

He was not going to let her back her way out of the corner into which he'd squeezed her. His expectant dark eyes remained focused on her face.

"Then I have no choice," Alexa said. There was obvious resignation in her voice. She finally accepted he wouldn't budge. It was his way or nothing.

She tried not to think about what she was agreeing to. To return to the mansion and live as Leonardo's wife again was difficult to accept. Most women would love the life of luxury she had lived, but she hated it. She hated the mansion, which she viewed as nothing more than a gilded cage.

Although she couldn't tell her brother what she planned to do, she hoped he appreciated the sacrifice she made in coming here in the first place.

"Then we have a deal."

His voice was filled with the satisfaction of a man who'd gotten the upper hand. Alexa watched Leonardo walk over to a file cabinet, unlock it, and pull out a large checkbook. He moved back to the desk and flipped to a blank check.

"What should I tell people when they ask—about our reconciliation?"

"Tell them we decided to try again. People love the idea of a reunion." He didn't seem particularly interested in the conversation or the explanations that would be required of them.

He leaned over the desk, his long, dark fingers gliding along the page as he wrote out the sum. With each stroke of the pen, Alexa felt as if a noose were tightening around her neck. Once she took the money, she was as good as his.

"How do I know you'll keep your word?" she asked. Although she'd never known Leonardo to renege on a promise, she had to be sure. It would be so easy for him to put a stop payment on the check and endanger her brother's future and make her into a liar. "Should there be some kind of contract?"

His fingers paused in the midst of endorsing the check.

"If anyone should ask for a contract, it's me," he said. He finished his name and then lifted his eyes from the book. "I've never had a problem with keeping my word. You, on the other hand"—he straightened, staring her down—"can't be trusted. Till death do us part. Remember that? You didn't exactly stick to your side of the deal, now did you?"

She should have just kept her mouth shut. Take the money and run.

"I had good reason," she said defensively.

"Is that right? What reason was that?"

It was foolish to engage in verbal sparring with Leo, but Alexa found she couldn't resist. She needed to answer his mocking questions, even if it didn't matter to him. "Our marriage wasn't what it should be. If you're honest with yourself, you'll agree neither of us got what we wanted out of it."

She didn't waver from his piercing appraisal, though it took monumental strength to maintain eye contact with him. He was used to making his opponents cower, but that particular intimidation tactic wouldn't work today. She'd had four months to rebuild her self-esteem, and she'd had plenty of time to brace herself for this meeting with him once she and Xander decided it was a necessity.

"Was it because I was working hard making millions of dollars to maintain our lifestyle and make sure you had the security most women could only dream of? Or was it because you could no longer go gallivanting around town with your friends, flitting from party to party because suddenly you had to behave like a wife instead of a woman with no responsibilities?"

His words couldn't have been farther from the truth. She'd never gallivanted in her life. She was the opposite of a social butterfly and resented that he made the few times she went out with her friends sound as if she were some kind of immature party girl. When she'd ventured out, it was because he was unavailable to join her. She spent more evenings out and about as his wife than she ever did as a single woman. There was always some party, charity function, or business dinner that required his presence.

If she didn't need the money so badly, she would tell him exactly what she thought of him, his hard work, and his erroneous claims about her social life.

Forcing herself to remain calm, Alexa took a deep breath and held out her hand. "I think you've insulted me enough for one day. If you hand me the check, I'll get out of your hair."

Leonardo just looked at her hand, the slim wrist, the delicate fingers. She thought he would ignore her. Just as she was about to pull back, he enveloped her small hand in one of his.

The warm clasp was like an electric shock to her system. The immediate effect of his touch left her breathless, dizzy. How could he still have this effect on her?

Leonardo lifted her hand to his lips, heating her flesh with the pressure of his mouth against the sensitive skin of her palm. It was impossible not to react, not to tremble as her breasts tightened and the intimate core of her body throbbed as if he'd pressed the kiss there instead.

He flicked the tip of his tongue against her hand, and she tried to pull back as tiny shivers trickled up her arm. He only tightened his grip.

"Let go," she whispered. She was fighting him as much as her body's reaction to his touch.

"Not yet."

Leonardo tugged, and she fell into him, her breasts crushed against his hard chest. He clamped his arm around her waist so she couldn't move. His eyes darkened as he felt her soft, supple body. That wasn't the only physical manifestation of his desire for her.

Alexa felt him harden against her stomach, and she was swamped with feelings that she hadn't felt in so long, her knees weakened.

He lowered his head to her neck and inhaled in deep appreciation of the flowery scent of her skin. The tip of his tongue traced a sensuous arch along the shell of her ear.

Alexa closed her eyes and felt her body melt into his, his heart thumping beneath her palms.

"I can't wait to get you back into bed," he said huskily.

His hand lowered to her bottom and squeezed the flesh with possessive fingers, kneading it in a way that brooked no argument that it was his right to do so.

Alexa resisted the urge to grind against him. Her body was on fire with unrestrained need that she'd locked away and held behind a façade of cool indifference.

"Maybe this time I won't let you leave."

Alexa's startled brown eyes locked with Leonardo's hard black ones. She tried to wrench herself from his grasp, but he wouldn't have it. He held her fast in an iron grip.

"You said two months," she reminded him. "You can't force me to stay with you indefinitely." She successfully disengaged herself from his arms. He coolly looked down at her from his superior height, as if the heated response of their bodies pressed against each other had never taken place. "It was a mistake for me to come here."

She grabbed her purse and rushed toward the door.

"You can have the check, Alexa," Leonardo called before she could make it to the door.

When she turned to face him, she saw he held the check in his outstretched hand. Her stomach was in knots, thinking about her brother and what she would say to him if she showed up without it.

"Two months, Leo, that's it." She spoke in a firm voice, disguising how upset she was.

"Two months, Alexa, and then you're free of me."

With as much dignity as she could muster, Alexa bumped up her chin and took the few strides back to Leonardo. She slipped the check from his fingers and moved to escape.

His voice halted her at the door. "No 'thank you'?" he taunted.

"We both know that's not how you expect me to show my appreciation," Alexa said woodenly. She stared at the dark oak door instead of turning to face him.

"Well, at least thank Xander, for getting my wife back for me, even if it's only temporary. By the way, he gets the check today, and you move back in tomorrow. I'll have my assistant call you to make the arrangements to have you move back into the house."

So soon. Of course he wouldn't waste any time, but still . . .

Alexa twisted the knob and hastily exited Leonardo's office.

* * *

Looking out over the Atlanta skyline, Leonardo's eyes narrowed.

He'd done it. That was how badly he wanted her. It didn't matter that it was unethical. He'd achieved the desired result— Alexa would be back in his home and back in his bed.

He applied pressure to his nape, to ease the tension from having her in his office. Despite his intention to do otherwise, he'd been incapable of making it through the brief meeting without touching her. She'd been too close. Her creamy skin, the color of café au lait, proved too much of a temptation. Her almond-shaped brown eyes had surveyed him with anger, but her displeasure did little to quench the hunger in his loins.

Leonardo compressed his teeth. Even now the fragrant scent of her skin along the slope of her neck lingered in his nostrils. He liked her new short haircut. He liked the way the full, bouncy curls curved into her neck. He couldn't wait to take a handful of her hair and feel the silken tresses slip through his fingers as he devoured her luscious, pouty mouth. That mouth.

Abruptly, Leonardo turned from the window to quell the arousing thoughts. He still wanted her to the point of distraction, and despite acting as if she were being sentenced to the guillotine, he knew she wanted him, too. There was no mistaking the way her body softened against his.

Sooner or later they would enjoy each other's bodies. As far as he was concerned, the sooner the better.

CHAPTER 3

*D*ownstairs, Alexa hailed a taxi and made her way over to her brother's apartment. She was suffering through a multitude of emotions. She was excited to tell him the good news, but she was bone weary from her trying ordeal with Leonardo. It had sapped more of her strength than she realized it would.

In the cab, she rested her head back and closed her eyes.

"Maybe this time I won't let you leave."

Alexa drew a shaky breath. She began to tremble, tremble because she suddenly longed to resume their marriage and give him what he wanted. Seeing him again had been jarring. She had felt the tug of physical attraction that had roped her in from the first day she met him. Being intimate with him was not something she expected would ever happen again, but the thought of it caused a longing in her body that was not only difficult to understand, it posed an unsettling distraction.

Alexa rummaged through her purse for her makeup. She would have to give the performance of an award-winning actress to convince Xander everything was fine, that she and Leonardo had decided to reconcile. Maybe it was because they were twins, but she and her brother had a sixth sense where each other was concerned. They could take one look at each other and determine if there was something wrong.

She reapplied the reddish-bronze color to her lips and ran her fingers through her wind-tousled ebony curls to tame them. She needed to look her best to convince her brother that all was right with the world. She didn't want him to feel guilty about how she came to get the money from Leonardo. Now he could pay his creditor and resume concentrating on the bakery instead of worrying about how he would take care of his wife and children.

Using her key, Alexa entered the townhouse Xander shared with his wife and four children. R & B music blared from the back, and that meant Xander was hard at work on one of his culinary creations.

"Xander!" she called out.

She made her way down the carpeted hall to the back, where the kitchen was. He looked up and smiled, hesitantly, when she entered. Just as she expected, he was leaning over the marble countertop of the island in the big kitchen, kneading a mountain of dough, his shirtsleeves rolled up and his forearms dusted with flour. The wait had taken its toll on him, as well, because he always baked when he was stressed.

He was slim, but muscular, and he shared similar facial features with Alexa. He was five feet eleven, and his brown eyes, in her opinion, were his best feature. She always teased him and told him he had kind puppy dog eyes.

"Turn the music down," Alexa said loudly, dropping her purse onto the barstool on the opposite side of the island from her brother.

Xander nodded and then walked over to the wall near the sink and turned off the radio mounted there. He washed his hands and then turned to face her again.

"Well?"

He looked so young and worried, Alexa felt her heart squeeze in her chest. It only served to confirm she had made the right decision.

Although they were only minutes apart, she often felt like the older, more mature sibling. Their parents passed away in a car accident just after their graduation, and Xander hadn't taken it well. She tried to be his rock, even though she grieved deeply herself. She'd been even more concerned when, only months later, he eloped to Las Vegas and married his high school sweetheart. Ten years and four children later, Xander was still happily married, despite his financial struggles. She, however, was headed for divorce. So much for being the more mature one.

"Good news," Alexa said brightly, beginning her performance. "He gave me a check."

Xander breathed a heavy sigh, flung his head backward, and cried out, "Yesss!" Without warning, he raced around the island and lifted Alexa from the floor, spinning her around in an exuberant hug.

She laughed. "Put me down!"

Dropping her to her feet, Xander looked at Alexa. "What did he say? How did he react? How did you convince him?" He was so excited his eyes were glowing with pleasure.

"Well . . ." Alexa hedged, making a show of getting up on the other barstool next to her purse. "It wasn't hard. He was very open to it, surprisingly enough. I didn't have to talk him into it."

Xander looked stunned. "He just said yes—just like that?" He snapped his fingers. "I can't believe it."

Alexa lifted one shoulder. "Just be thankful he was in a generous mood."

"See, I told you there was nothing to worry about," Xander said, hitting her lightly in the arm with his fist. "So, what are the terms?"

"You're not gonna believe this," Alexa began, "but you don't have to pay him back. Consider it a gift."

The room grew quiet as Xander digested this bit of information. "Wait a minute. That doesn't make sense, Lexie." A frown of worry creased his brow. "Why would he do that? Leo's a businessman. Why would he just give me almost a quarter of a million dollars?"

"He doesn't need the money, Xander. It's a drop in the bucket for him. Besides, you're my brother, and he's always liked you. I think he just wanted to help, that's all." She punched him in the shoulder this time, trying to make light of the situation before he realized there was more to it than what she said. "Isn't that why you asked me to go instead of you—to make sure you got the money? I'm just a better negotiator than you realized, that's all."

Xander eyed her for a moment, then said, "Don't think I don't appreciate what you did, but I'm not a charity case. I can pay Leo back. I just couldn't afford to pay the note in full. I was going to lose everything."

A cloud seemed to settle over his face as he thought about how he could have lost the bakery once the finance company accelerated the loan. Alexa knew it upset him that he'd been so careless. The fact of the matter was, Xander didn't have a head for business, and it was time he admitted it and got help.

"Xander, he did have one stipulation to releasing the funds." Well, two, but she would only mention one. Alexa pulled the check from her purse. "He insists that you get an office manager, and I have to agree with him."

Xander groaned. "Are you kidding me? Why would I want someone else in my personal business—"

"You don't have a choice. You missed payments on your business loan, Xander. That's why the finance company accelerated the loan payment."

Xander cursed. "I still don't understand why they would do that. The bakery's doing well. I just missed a couple of payments."

And the reminder notices they sent, Alexa thought. He also didn't pay the electric bill at one point, resulting in a car-screeching dash to the power company so the bakery could be opened on time.

Alexa refrained from reminding him of that episode and all the other incidents she knew about.

"They have a right to do it. It's written in the contract, so they exercised their right." Alexa had been surprised, as well, but the clause was right there in black and white. It was a typical stipulation lenders included in loan paperwork. Xander had initialed right next to it.

"Now I have to get an office manager," Xander grumbled.

"Yes, or you don't get the check." Alexa tilted her head. "Would you look at the bright side and stop pouting? You just got free money, and all you have to do is get someone to help you manage it."

A guilty smile came over Xander's face. "Sorry about that. I'm being a jerk." He kissed her on the cheek, and she handed him the check. Looking down at it in awe, he said, "It must be nice to be able to just write a check like this and not have it put a dent in your finances." He glanced up at Alexa.

"Man, I really owe Leo big time." Suddenly, his face lit up. "Holy crap! I didn't even ask you what happened when you two saw each other again. Did you talk about anything besides the loan—I mean, gift?"

This was the perfect opening to tell Xander about the "reconciliation" with Leonardo.

She had never fully explained the reason for her separation from Leonardo. All she'd told Xander was that they decided to go their separate ways because they found they were no longer compatible. He had no idea how insecure she'd felt or the depth of her aloneness as his wife.

"Well, as a matter of fact, things went really well." Alexa forced a smile to her lips that she hoped looked genuine. "Leo and I talked, and we're getting back together. I'm moving back into the house tomorrow."

Xander's eyes widened to the size of dinner plates.

Alexa kept talking, as he remained speechless. "He wanted . . . me back, and I recognized that it was a good thing I'd gone up there instead of you, or he and I would never have . . . realized how we felt about each other." She stopped looking at him long before she finished the difficult sentence. It was always hard to be dishonest with her brother.

The tick-tock of the clock was loud in the quiet kitchen.

"Lexie—"

"Xander, everything worked out. You got the money, and Leo and I are getting back together again." She had to stop him from prying, because she knew it was coming. He suspected, just as she knew he would, that something was wrong.

Another fake, bright smile was plastered on her face.

Xander looked down at the check. He didn't look happy. He looked uncomfortable, concerned.

"Lexie," he began again. "I appreciate—"

"You're welcome," Alexa interjected. She hopped down off the barstool and lifted her purse over her shoulder. "I just came by to give you the check and my good news. I've gotta run because I have a million things to do before I move back in with Leo."

"Lexie, wait, just listen for a minute."

Alexa touched her palm to her brother's cheek. "Stop thinking so much," she whispered. "You got what you needed. It was nothing. You're my brother, and I'd do anything for you."

"I don't want you to do *anything* for me." He placed the check on the counter. He wouldn't look at her. "I should've gone myself, instead of you. Leo can be so intimidating sometimes. I just thought since you two were married . . ."

Alexa touched his arm and brought his attention back to her. "Xander, you're back on track. Just make sure you keep baking

24

those wonderful treats, and make sure you hire an office manager."

Xander nodded. "Yeah, I obviously don't have a head for managing a business," he said sheepishly. Playfully, he reached out and tweaked Alexa's nose with the knuckles of his forefinger and middle finger. "You're sure everything's fine?" His voice held a hint of humor, but his eyes were watching her closely.

She couldn't allow him to feel guilty. She wanted him to jump back into the business without any worries. Leonardo was her problem, not his.

"Couldn't be better," she lied, ignoring the guilt in favor of telling herself there was a good reason for it: she was helping her brother and the five other people who depended on him.

The tension eased somewhat from his shoulders, and Alexa knew her job was done.

"I'll send the two of you a special cake," Xander announced, following Alexa out of the kitchen toward the front of the house. "I'll create something really nice just for the two of you to celebrate getting back together and to thank Leo for what he's done for me and my family."

"I'm sure he'll appreciate it, Xander, but don't go to too much trouble. Leo will be happy with a simple 'thank you.'"

They hugged at the door before Alexa took off down the sidewalk to a coffee shop a few blocks away from her brother's home. She entered the shop and placed her order. Then she sat down in a corner with the hot brew. It gave her time to think, to escape reality for a while. Chewing on her lower lip, she made a silent request for forgiveness for not being completely honest with her brother. In the end, her actions would benefit him and his family. Her temporary return to Leonardo was a small sacrifice.

Alexa took a sip and allowed herself to drift back into the past and one of the arguments that had taken place not long before she made the decision to leave him for good. Leaving him was the hardest decision she'd ever made. She had loved her husband, but it was clear she was only secondary in his life. His business was his real wife.

* * *

"A BABY IS out of the question. We've already had this conversation!" Alexa fumed. She stormed onto the balcony outside the master suite, barefoot but still elegantly attired in her black cocktail dress and the exquisite diamonds that graced her neck and adorned her ears.

She'd smiled and entertained more of Leonardo's business associates who'd come to the house for dinner. She couldn't remember the last time they'd actually had people over for fun, just for a dinner party that didn't involve making a good impression so that millions of dollars could be transferred between large bank accounts.

The only reason he'd broached the topic again was because one of his guests had pulled out what could only be described as a mini photo album of his five-month-old son. The proud father had passed around the photos during the after-dinner drinks, and she'd known, as soon as they left, Leonardo would broach the topic of children again.

It wasn't that she didn't want children. She did. She longed for children of her own, in fact. But how could she bring children into their frayed marriage? How could she, when she herself knew what it was like to suffer through the pain of hearing her parents fight on an almost daily basis, and knowing how difficult it had been growing up never seeing her own father as he worked no less than a hundred hours per week running his bakery?

Been there, done that. It would be selfish to repeat the sins of her own parents and make her child suffer through the feelings of neglect she and Xander experienced growing up. The only good thing that came out of her dysfunctional family was the closeness she and Xander shared. They were downright inseparable.

Leonardo followed more slowly, no longer wearing his tuxedo jacket. The sleeves of his white shirt were rolled up onto bronze forearms sprinkled with fine, wiry hairs. He stood behind her as she looked down over the private courtyard. He placed one hand on the railing on either side of her, imprisoning her so she couldn't get away from his words.

"We never talk about it, Alexa. You yell and stomp around. Then I'm left to wonder why there doesn't seem to be a maternal bone in your body—something I completely missed before I married you."

Alexa winced, happy for the darkness of the balcony and the fact that he stood behind her so he couldn't read in her face the pain his words caused. Contrary to what he believed, she did have maternal tendencies. She enjoyed spending time with her nieces and nephews, and before their marriage, she was the go-to babysitter when Xander and his wife wanted a night out.

She could tell him the reason she didn't want to have a child, but he wouldn't understand. It would sound like she was nagging him, complaining about his work again when that was what allowed her to live in their luxurious lifestyle. She'd stopped complaining a while back, hating how she sounded. She didn't want to turn into her mother, so she didn't explain.

"You missed a lot. You were too focused on trying to get me into bed with you."

That was probably the only reason why they were married. Because she'd had the fortitude to resist his persistent charm, they hadn't made love until after they were married.

His hands roamed up her thighs and settled on her hips. She tried not to react, but it was impossible, and she knew this argument would end the way they always did—in bed, with no resolution.

"Do you blame me?" He pressed his lips against the soft skin of her bare back. "I've wanted you ever since I saw you in that boutique, and I knew I had to have you." His hands slipped in front so that his fingers could splay across her flat stomach.

He never said the word "love." "Want" and "need" were the only words in his vocabulary when he referred to her or their relationship. Before, she'd thought it would be enough, because she understood he was the type of man who never found occasion to express his emotions. But it wasn't enough. It wasn't, because she loved him and wanted to hear him say he loved her.

She ached to be closer to him and spend more time with him, and all he cared about were spreadsheets and dollar signs. She didn't mean nearly as much to him as he did to her. It was the experience of her childhood all over again.

His hands exerted pressure and eased her back against his aroused body. "I want a child, our child, and brothers and sisters for him or her. I need you to understand that and how important it is to me."

Alexa shifted away from him, pushing his hands away from her. He could so easily make her weak, so easily make her behave in an irrational way, no matter how much she thought through a decision. She wanted to remain rational tonight, because his seductive touch was meant to convince her to change her mind.

Licking her dry lips, she turned to face him. "I said no, Leo." Her voice was firm. "I don't want a child right now."

His body grew very still. Looking deeply into her eyes, he asked, "Then when?"

"I . . . I don't know," she stammered. "I need time to think about it."

"You're stalling."

"No, I'm not." Alexa stepped away from Leonardo.

He didn't let her escape that easily. One large hand grasped her waist and pulled her closer. He inched the hem of her dress up her thigh. "No matter. One thing at a time," he murmured against the corner of her mouth. "Right now, all I care about is getting you out of this."

ALEXA CAME BACK to the present with a start. No point in letting her mind wander in that direction. She had plenty to deal with before entering back into the life she had with her husband. Sighing, she placed her now empty cup in the trash and flipped open her phone to call another taxi.

CHAPTER 4

*A*lexa pulled open the door to Second Chance Closet, a charity she had formed, located in midtown Atlanta.

Despite losing their parents at a young age, both Xander and Alexa had learned the value of going into business for themselves. She had opened a boutique selling women and children's clothing and accessories. He followed in their father's footsteps and opened a bakery.

Not long after her marriage to Leonardo, Alexa sold her half of the boutique to her business partner. Longing to do something more meaningful, she started the charity with the proceeds she earned from the sale. The store provided gently used career clothing and formal wear to women.

Working with the women's shelters, a prison outreach program, and government assistance programs, Alexa accepted vouchers that were used to "purchase" clothing for various occasions, giving women who otherwise wouldn't be able to afford these clothes the opportunity to make a good first impression. For regular customers looking for a good deal, the clothing items could be purchased with money, which helped to fund the program.

Donations were solicited from various sources, and Alexa herself had donated a number of her evening gowns to be sold, since being Leonardo's wife meant she seldom wore the same designer outfit twice.

She greeted the older woman behind the cash register. "Hi, Edna." She had hired Edna to work full-time, and there were also a couple of part-time volunteers. The Closet, as they referred to the five-thousand-square-foot store, had made quite a splash in the Atlanta area, and Alexa proudly displayed framed newspaper and magazine clippings on the wall behind the counter. They extolled the impact the store made on the morale and lives of the recipients of the clothing.

The store would be closing soon for the day, so it was empty except for Edna.

"Hi, Alexa," Edna said, smiling. "I didn't expect you in this afternoon."

"I'm just going back to the office for a few minutes to check on some things since I won't be coming by tomorrow." On her way over, Alexa decided it would be best to concentrate her time tomorrow on reacclimating herself back into her life as Leonardo's wife.

She noticed boxes stacked in the corner. "I see Ms. Johnson brought by her donation as promised."

Ms. Johnson was an attorney who was retiring from her profession and had promised Alexa she would donate all her business suits and dresses to Second Chance Closet. Alexa was excited to see the boxes because so many women would benefit from the contents.

Edna nodded. "Her son dropped them off just before you got here. You just missed him. I'll get one of the girls to help me with the inventory next week."

"Sounds good. Whenever you get finished here, feel free to go on home. I'll lock up."

Alexa then went toward the back office she shared with

Edna. After sitting down in the chair behind the desk, she tapped the keyboard and took a look at the inventory for the week.

"Not bad," she murmured.

Smaller donations arrived a couple of times during the week, and Edna had already noted in the system who the donations were from and that they needed a thank-you card sent to them. She added Ms. Johnson's name to the list. Showing their appreciation served to not only encourage donors to donate again in the future, but it also gave them a good mailing list to work from when soliciting for special events and additional donations.

Alexa clicked through the data on the screen, noting the number of vouchers that had been redeemed. Her train of thought was interrupted when the phone on the desk rang, indicating Edna had transferred a call to her.

"Hello, Alexa," Leonardo said in his smooth voice, the slightly accented pronunciation of her name creating goose bumps along her arms. "Have you already been to see your brother?"

His unexpected call diverted her attention away from the computer screen. "Yes, I have. He was very appreciative of what you did for him."

"It was my pleasure."

Alexa thought she detected a smile in his voice. When she told Xander that Leonardo liked him, it hadn't been an untruth. Leonardo did like his enthusiasm for his work, and at times she thought he saw Xander as the younger brother he never had.

"I wanted to let you know that I have an invitation to Russell and Joan's anniversary party taking place tomorrow evening. They've invited about a hundred or so people to their home. I thought it would be a good idea for us to go out together and let everyone see that we're back together again."

Alexa stopped her nervous twiddling of the pen in her hand.

She didn't want to go to a party with Leonardo because she didn't feel up to smiling and pretending they were a happily reunited couple. It would be even harder because she really liked Joan and Russell and had considered them friends when she and Leonardo were together. She would have to be cautious about how she turned him down.

"I can't," she responded.

"Why not?" She could hear the arrogance in his voice, as if she should drop whatever it is to join him tomorrow night.

"I'm busy. I have to get settled in."

"That's a nonissue," Leonardo informed her. "One of the servants can unpack your bags, and my assistant is taking care of the logistics. She'll be calling you later tonight with the details."

Making one more attempt to get out of the invitation, Alexa said, "It's not a good time. It's the end of the month, and I need to review the books for The Closet. Not to mention I'll have to find something to wear, and I'm not so sure it's a good idea for us to be seen together so soon. Do you really think I'm that good of an actress? Are you that great of an actor?" There. She'd said it. Neither of them could pretend that well under the scrutiny of dozens of other people.

"It wasn't a request, Alexa."

She allowed silence to remain on the line for a few moments. Of course it wasn't. Leonardo was in control, and he wouldn't take no for an answer. "Just drop whatever I have planned?"

"Precisely."

"Is that what I can expect moving forward? This can't go on indefinitely."

"It won't. As you reminded me before you left, it's only for two months."

"Fine. Since I don't have a choice." She wanted to sound angry, but instead her voice came out weaker than she intended. For some ridiculous reason, having him remind her that they were only back together for a short while made Alexa unhappy.

"You always have a choice. You had a choice of whether or not you should come back to me, and you chose to do so. I didn't force you."

She held back the laugh that threatened to ripple from down deep in her throat. How could two people have such disparate views of the same situation?

"I still have to find a dress," Alexa said. "There isn't much time. I'd have to spend all of tomorrow shopping if I'm going to find something appropriate to wear to the Simpsons' party."

"There's no need to be concerned about what you'll wear tomorrow," Leonardo said in a brisk voice, which was an indication he was ready to wrap up the conversation. "Everything you need is at the house. So you'll join me tomorrow? I think everyone will enjoy seeing you and be pleased that we've reconciled."

Except that they weren't reconciled. It was a lie.

Alexa bit back the angry retort that hovered around her lips. Instead, she kept her voice neutral when she spoke again. "I'll join you tomorrow night. I'll go along with your charade for the next two months, Leo. I'll go to your parties, act like the perfect hostess when you throw your own, and run your home the way you like. But as soon as the time is up, I'm walking away as quickly as I can."

"Don't forget you'll also have to share my bed every night," Leonardo said.

Alexa felt her pulse flutter. Of course he would remind her of that part.

"I will see you tomorrow night at home," he added.

At home.

Alexa froze as her neck muscles tensed. The words left his tongue with ease, but for her, it was difficult to imagine the sprawling mansion as home. It hadn't been home for some time, and she wondered what it would feel like to be back there and if anything had changed. No doubt Leonardo had worked to eradicate from every corner any evidence she had ever lived there.

"I'll see you tomorrow, Leo."

* * *

THE WELL-TENDED LAWN and shrubs looked the same when the chauffeured car Leonardo sent for Alexa cruised through the iron gates and made its way up the winding cobblestone driveway made of granite pavers. The grass looked like a soft green carpet, and the shrubs were rounded and trimmed into neat cylindrical shapes. Even the rose bushes she'd requested the gardener plant were still in place on either side of the imposing front door, adding a vivid splash of color against the stucco walls.

Upon entering the house, Alexa found that the furnishings and décor were exactly the same, too. She didn't know if that was a good thing or not. Because her surroundings were identical to when she left, she felt her old apprehensions resurfacing. She was back in the same imposing house she had fled because she was so unhappy.

"Good afternoon, Mrs. Silva."

The housekeeper greeted her with a smile when their paths crossed. Because of the housekeeper, the maids, the house manager, the butler, the cook, the gardeners, the pool man, and the chauffeur, the mansion operated like a Fortune 500 company. When Alexa lived there, her role as the woman of the house was to manage the staff, but they were so efficient she often felt superfluous.

Alexa returned the housekeeper's greeting. If she was surprised to see Alexa, she gave no indication, and neither did the other employees. Everyone behaved as if she had never left. It made her wonder what exactly Leonardo had said to them.

She took her time up the stairs to the room she would once again share with her husband. The master bedroom suite was at the end of a hallway in the east wing of the house. The balcony leading off of it overlooked a swimming pool. Concrete steps led from the balcony to the private courtyard below.

The main room was minimally furnished, with a large king-size bed in its center, a wall-mounted flatscreen television, two nightstands, and expensive original paintings from several contemporary artists hanging on the walls. A sitting room complete with large cushioned chairs was off to the side.

It also included a desk, chair, and a networked laptop and printer so Leonardo could work late at night if he chose to without having to go to his office on the ground floor.

Three doors opened into two large walk-in closets and a gigantic bathroom decorated with slate gray imported Italian marble tile, a jetted tub, and two sinks.

Leonardo's assistant had arranged for Alexa's luggage to be brought to the house, but she didn't see her personal belongings in the room when she entered. She assumed one of the servants had already unpacked her few bags and put away her things. She walked over to the closet that used to be hers before she left—and gasped.

Alexa stood immobile in front of the immense closet, staring at the contents in disbelief. The built-in shelves and hangers were filled almost to capacity. Everything she'd left behind was still there: the designer clothes, shoes, handbags, accessories—everything. No wonder he'd seemed unconcerned about whether or not she'd have something to wear tonight.

The closet doubled as a dressing room, with a vanity and mirror in a corner, and a full-length mirror nestled between shelves that held neatly arranged shoes and boots. She opened several drawers and discovered more clothes, undergarments, lingerie, all neatly folded where she had left them. It was almost eerie how perfect everything remained, as if she'd never left—or as if he'd known she would be back.

Her one-of-a-kind jewelry box dominated one of the shelves where she'd left it and the contents. Other pieces were locked in the safe. She hadn't left with any of the jewelry or clothing Leonardo had given to her, although she knew it was rightfully hers. It was obvious if she did an inventory of what was still there, she would find not one single item had been removed.

A faint sound made her swing around. Alexa found herself face-to-face with Leonardo in the suddenly confining space.

"Don't look so frightened." He began tugging on his striped tie as he spoke. "I don't plan to maul you."

Alexa licked her suddenly dry lips, focusing on his face instead of allowing her gaze to drift down to the smooth, swarthy skin of the newly exposed column of his neck. She was embarrassed by her instinctive reaction to his small movement.

"It's the middle of the afternoon. I didn't expect you home so soon."

He couldn't seem to take his black gaze from her moistened lips, and Alexa felt the shimmer of awareness hum between them.

"I wrapped up a business deal sooner than expected. When you're the boss, you can leave work early."

Alexa wanted to ask if he had a habit of leaving work early nowadays, but she didn't. Before they separated, she hardly ever saw him before the middle of the night. She couldn't count the number of nights she ate dinner alone. On the days when he did arrive early, after they made love, he would work in the sitting room or shut himself in his office so that she was forced to entertain herself.

With a short hand gesture, Alexa indicated the contents of the closet. "I thought you would throw everything out once I left. Why didn't you?"

Leonardo didn't answer right away. He strolled over to the far side of the closet, where the jewelry box was located.

"Sentimental reasons," he said, his voice laced with cutthroat sarcasm. He lifted the top of the box and pulled something out. "You forgot these when you left." He held out his open palm to Alexa.

Her stomach tumbled over itself when she saw what he held. The large diamond in his palm captured the overhead light. The matching platinum wedding band lay nestled next to it.

"I didn't forget them," Alexa responded, barely above a whisper. The painful constriction of her chest made it difficult to speak.

She stared at the jewelry. She left them because she hadn't wanted a reminder of her marriage, which to her was already over. She also wanted to make a point of showing Leonardo how serious she was about leaving him. At the time, she never knew she would be back here again, still married to him.

"I didn't think you did," Leonardo admitted. He made his way over to her. "Give me your hand."

"Do we really have to do this?" Alexa asked. It was ridiculous, but she felt once she put the rings back on, her surrender to him would be complete, his control over her irrefutable.

"Yes." He smiled, but it didn't reach his eyes. "It's an important part of convincing everyone that we're back together again." He reached for her hand.

Alexa pulled back. "I can put them on myself."

Leonardo grabbed her hand anyway. He shoved the wedding ring onto her finger.

"Leo, I can do it myself." Her fingers shook slightly. The warmth of his touch sent her emotions into a tailspin.

His lips compressed into a thin line, and his grip on her wrist tightened, a clear indication he heard what she said but had no intention of honoring her request.

"Are you afraid of me?" The diamond followed, sliding easily onto her finger.

"No. I just don't want you to touch me!" Alexa pulled away, her back connecting with a row of shelves behind her. She needed to get away from him. The closet, bigger than the average person's bedroom, was ridiculously small with him in it.

His dark eyes glittered down at her. "Well, that's going to be a problem, isn't it? Considering our arrangement most definitely includes periods of me touching you."

There was that word again.

Arrangement.

That's what this farce of a marriage had been reduced to. She shouldn't be here, pretending everything was back to normal. But here she was, with her husband, with her rings on her finger, and she would have to feign normalcy for outside observers.

She was back in the house, but not because he loved her or couldn't live without her. In fact, four months had passed, and not once had he called or come after her. She'd waited, hoped, and he'd never called. Instead, when presented with a chance, he took the opportunity to teach her a lesson and satisfy his lust for her at the same time.

"I shouldn't have agreed to this." Alexa's voice was tight, strained.

"It's too late for regrets." Leonardo prowled closer, crowding her against the shelves without touching. "You're here now."

"I don't belong here." Alexa glanced around the closet, taking in the extravagant design, intricate woodwork, the clothes, all symbols of his wealth.

Her upbringing had been in an upper middle-class neighborhood, and she'd been a business owner for a few years before her partner bought her out. Still, there were times she found Leonardo's lifestyle so out of her league it was intimidating. When she looked at him again, the muscles in her throat tightened even more. "I never belonged here, and you know it. I was different, that was all."

A shocked look came into his eyes. "Is that what you think? That I married you because you were different?"

"Yes. Why else? I'm sure our ethnic differences were enough of a novelty to be intriguing. That didn't last, though. As the weeks wore on, it became more and more evident how much I didn't belong, and that maybe you even regretted it."

His eyes widened. "When did I ever tell you I regretted marrying you?"

Alexa promptly answered, ready to prove to him how correct she was, even if he wouldn't admit it outright. "You never came right out and said that, but it was obvious you regretted our marriage.

"You were hardly ever here. Your hours at work became longer and longer. And the women . . ." Her voice trailed off miserably. That was the hardest part. She never actually caught him doing anything wrong, but she had her suspicions.

"What women?" Leonardo ground out. "What regret? If anyone regretted our marriage, it was you. You ran away from me because it wasn't what you thought. Isn't that right?"

"No, it wasn't what I thought!" Alexa was gripped with the need to explain. "I didn't think I would be ignored by my own husband!"

"I wasn't ignoring you," Leonardo said testily. "I was busy, working. You had everything you wanted. I gave you a generous allowance. You had a car at your disposal, a beautiful home, jewelry, everything a woman wants."

Not everything, Alexa thought. "I never thought I'd have to fight for your attention."

"You never had to fight for my attention. You always had it." Leonardo ran a weary hand through his hair, ruffling the chestnut locks. "Why didn't you tell me you felt this way before?"

Alexa looked into his dark, emotion-filled eyes and tried to read what she saw there. She couldn't. He was a master at hiding his true feelings whenever he needed to.

"Would it have made a difference? Would it have stopped you from pursuing your business deals or stopped you from ignoring me and flirting with the beautiful women who caught your attention at every function you dragged me to?"

His eyes narrowed. "I never flirted. You clearly have a very active imagination." His gaze traveled over her chic, well-fitting clothes, as if reminding himself of what was beneath. "From the moment I saw you, there was never anyone else."

"Do you really expect me to believe that?"

He didn't know, but she'd seen him leaving a restaurant with another woman, on a night he was supposed to be working late. She watched from the cab as they parted ways, his arm resting against the small of her back as he helped her into her car. He had told her he would be working, but he had lied. He'd been enjoying dinner with the striking redhead.

Alexa glanced away as the pain of the memory lanced through her.

Leonardo sighed heavily, frustrated by the turn of the conversation. He closed his eyes briefly. When he looked at her again, he seemed to have calmed himself.

"I don't care what you think anymore, Alexa." He completely removed his tie and bunched the silk into a fist. "Whatever was wrong, you were the one who left, without giving me a chance to rectify what you *thought* I'd done wrong. That's how much our marriage meant to you."

When she opened her mouth to speak, he cut her off.

"Whatever you thought, it's in the past. All I care about is what we do from here on out—what you agreed to in my office yesterday. Do you remember that conversation?"

Alexa's mouth clamped shut. It was too difficult to answer, to admit what she'd agreed to. She wished she could forget.

"Let me remind you," Leonardo continued. "You agreed to spend the next two months with me, living as my wife, in every sense of the word."

She let out a shaky breath. "I haven't forgotten."

She wanted him, despite the anger and the pain that had resurfaced. He was just too good-looking, too tempting to resist. And he wanted her, too. She knew it as sure as she knew her own name. He liked sex, and he was incredibly good at it.

"Good." With a satisfied gleam in his eye, Leonardo turned on his heel toward the door. "Someone from your favorite spa will be here in about an hour to do your nails and makeup," he said over his shoulder. His footsteps halted at the door, and he turned fully to face her. "Wear the green dress you bought on our honeymoon in Paris." His eyes easily found the dress hanging from a hanger on the opposite wall. "I never got the pleasure of seeing you in it. We can rectify that tonight."

After he left, Alexa took a good look at the dress. She'd purchased it to wear on the last night of their honeymoon. He never saw her in it because their last night in Paris, when they were supposed to go out to dinner, he'd tied her to the bed. After their mind-blowing lovemaking, they'd ordered room service and eaten in the suite instead of venturing outdoors. Then they'd resumed their marathon session late into the night, loath to return to the routine of daily life they'd left behind.

Alexa wasn't a prude, but she felt her cheeks heat up anyway at the memory of the things Leonardo had done to her while she was bound to the bed in the hotel. Just thinking about it made her breathless.

If just the mere memory of his lovemaking could have her so shaken, how in the world would she be able to handle what was to come and leave intact in two months' time?

* * *

COOL WATER from the massaging showerhead trickled down Leonardo's body as the conversation with Alexa rewound in his mind.

When did she start thinking he was involved with other women? Had she always been so insecure? He hadn't noticed. Had he really been so preoccupied with work? She'd always been the epitome of self-confidence.

It's true she was different to him, but not in the way she'd indicated. The fact that she was African-American didn't have any bearing on his interest in her. He simply never considered ethnicity when he saw her. What made her different wasn't her race, but it was her personality, her beauty, and how she carried herself with quiet confidence and grace.

He noticed her right away, in the boutique she co-owned with a friend at the time. After she helped him pick out a gift for his assistant, he found he couldn't get her out of his mind and returned the same day to ask her out. After that initial date, he'd been sure that he would make her his wife.

Nothing would stand in his way.

She had been different in other ways, too. Unlike other women he'd known, she didn't seem impressed by his wealth, and she never appeared to want anything from him. Her lack of interest was refreshing, and he wanted to give her everything her heart desired, anything to make her happy.

Maybe that was his mistake. She never asked him for anything because she didn't want possessions.

Leonardo stopped the flow of water and reached for a towel on the warming rack.

He wasn't a man who dwelt on what-ifs and what could have been. He tried to learn from the past, because it couldn't be changed. With that in mind, he figured since he couldn't change what transpired between him and Alexa before, he would work on improving the future.

CHAPTER 5

$\mathcal{I}$nstead of having the driver take them to their destination, Leonardo decided to drive. The silver exterior of the vintage two-seater 1958 Porsche Speedster glowed in the dark night. The car was a prized possession. The moment he saw it, he knew he had to have it no matter the cost. He didn't often drive it, but it brought him pleasure when he did.

The engine roared to life once Alexa was buckled in and settled comfortably into the seat. She crossed her legs and proceeded to stare straight ahead.

Leonardo cast a sidelong glance in her direction.

He watched as she smoothed her fingers over the jeweled clutch on her lap. The silk material of the emerald green dress covered her body like a second layer of skin, emphasizing her narrow waist and full breasts. A split rose to midthigh and afforded a tempting view of her shapely leg.

His grip on the steering wheel tightened. He was acutely aware of every sound she made and every movement of her graceful body.

He wanted her. Badly. His loins ached with the need to possess her. He had been two seconds away from pressing her back against the bedroom wall when she'd emerged from the dressing room earlier. It would have been so easy for him to undo the gold clasp of the dress draped over her right shoulder and allow the soft material to fall away so he could feast his mouth on those tantalizing breasts that had haunted his dreams for the past four months.

Somehow he'd managed to rein in his actions much better than yesterday. The same rigid control he exercised in business had enabled him to maintain control over his actions and postpone what he had planned until later.

It had been difficult, though. It was always difficult with Alexa. He found it nearly impossible to keep his body in check when it came to her, and there didn't seem to be a thing he could do about it.

Leonardo turned to her. She wore makeup, but not much, because she didn't need it. There was no need to spoil her defined cheekbones with blush. Her smooth, honey-colored skin had a healthy glow, and her full lips were moist from the flattering pale color that graced them. Her jet-black hair was straight and brushed back from her face, styled a little higher on the top. She looked sexy and stylish, but sat rigidly in the seat.

"You look stiff." He shifted gears and returned his eyes to the road ahead.

"I'm sorry if my appearance doesn't please you. I'm sure I made it clear I didn't want to go out tonight." Her voice was cool, but that didn't stop him from having a very heated response to it.

* * *

LEONARDO TURNED the wheel slightly to shift lanes and speed past the car in front of them. "I didn't say your appearance doesn't please me. I said you look stiff. I hope you relax before we get there."

"I'll be fine. I'm just a little nervous," Alexa admitted.

A few seconds elapsed before he responded. "About what?"

Alexa twisted her head toward him. "About tonight. Everything. How much do these people know about our relationship, Leo? Most of them are your friends. What kind of reception can I expect?"

"I don't know who all the guests will be, but you know Russell and Joan. They adore you."

She turned away again and began to chew on the inside of her lower lip. Before she'd said the words, she didn't even realize just how nervous she was, and she certainly hadn't intended to admit as much to Leonardo.

"Stop doing that."

"What?"

His eyes found hers in the dimly lit vehicle. "Biting the inside of your lip." His words weren't harsh. In fact, they were gently spoken. He wasn't chastising her. "You have nothing to worry about. Russell and Joan like you. All anyone knows is that we went through a separation, and that's it. No details. Rest assured I never once said a bad word about you. Once we get there, you'll realize just how ridiculous your concerns are."

In an unexpected move, he reached across and covered her fingers with the warmth of his hand.

The touch made her skin tingle, but there was something else, too. It was a comforting gesture, and Alexa felt tears spring to her eyes. The tenderness of his touch threatened to undo her, and she didn't want to fall apart, start crying, and ruin her makeup. She appreciated his attempt to boost her confidence, because she'd only just recognized herself the true reason for her unease in attending the party tonight.

How could the hardened, unfeeling man she went to

yesterday be the same man providing comfort and assurance in her time of need? Why hadn't he before they were separated? Had he simply not understood the depth of her concerns all along?

Being apart for the past four months had done nothing to squash the feelings that blossomed inside of her whenever he was near. She hadn't wanted to admit it, but working at Second Chance Closet and helping her brother with the bakery became welcome diversions from dealing with her broken marriage. She'd told herself it was for the best and eventually she would get over it. She'd even convinced herself she no longer loved him and the time away had been good.

She was no longer deceived. Just over twenty-four hours after thrusting herself back into Leonardo's life, she found she was wishing their temporary arrangement could become permanent.

* * *

RUSSELL SIMPSON WAS a successful corporate attorney whose firm worked closely with Leonardo on Radiant Communications' telecommunications licensing deals. Over time they'd become very good friends and usually shared in the milestones in each other's lives. Tonight, Russell and his wife, Joan, were celebrating their thirtieth anniversary.

The two were complete opposites, but they managed to make it work. Where he was reserved, she was outgoing. He was conservative, and she was liberal. He was a Yankee from New York, and she was a born and bred Southern gal from Rome, Georgia. Yet, they were perfect together, and thirty years of marriage hadn't changed that one bit.

The Simpsons' home was located in an exclusive gated community in a suburb of Atlanta. Theirs was one of the few homes situated on the lake. Standing outside the door was a group of attendants hired to take care of the guests.

After the Porsche was driven away by the attending valet, another young man escorted Alexa and Leonardo into the house, through the grand foyer, and down a hall to the room where the anniversary party was in full swing.

Several large stations were set up with food for guests to help themselves. There was a hot table, a cold table, and a dessert table. Meanwhile, uniformed servers circulated with glasses of wine and champagne and even more food to nibble on. In one corner was a bar with an attending bartender making mixed drinks. Tables and chairs were strategically arranged in the room to encourage conversations of two or three. Two beautiful Strass crystal chandeliers punctuated the elegance of the room and its high-end decorations.

After a short while, Alexa was surprised how easy it was to fall back into her old routine as she mingled with the other guests. She was proud to stand beside Leonardo and be intro-duced as his wife. He was handsome in his well-fitting tuxedo, his wavy dark brown hair tamed and brushed back from his face, resting across his collar.

They spent the next forty minutes or so chatting with the other guests. From time to time, they were drawn into sepa-rate conversations, mostly because Leonardo was pulled away to talk business. He never strayed too far or too long, and Alexa wondered if he was doing it on purpose—purposely returning to her side so she wouldn't feel uncomfortable or alone. She wouldn't be surprised, not since he'd shown her such gentleness in the car. Part of her warmed to the thought that he was being so considerate, and her resolve to remain cool and distant melted against the warmth of his atten-tiveness.

"Well, hello!" That high-pitched Southern twang could belong to none other than Joan Simpson.

Alexa turned just in time to be drawn into the older woman's warm embrace. "Do my eyes deceive me?"

Alexa returned the hug. "No," she said, smiling into Joan's stunned face. Joan had been friendly from the first time they met, and this meeting reminded Alexa of how welcoming she was and how much she had missed the camaraderie when she left Leonardo.

"What's going on here?" Joan asked, eyeing one and then the other. She propped her hand on her hip and tilted back her platinum blonde head to give Leonardo a questioning look.

Leonardo's arm snaked around Alexa's waist and drew her close to his side. The intimate gesture made her body tingle in hidden places. "What does it look like?" he asked with a roguish grin.

"It looks like you two are back together," Joan answered, looking as if she'd just learned a juicy bit of gossip and couldn't wait to get permission to spread it around the neighborhood.

"Then you would be right." Leonardo's fingers moved slightly up and down Alexa's side and came to rest on her hip. She wondered if he had any idea the havoc he was wreaking with such innocent physical contact.

"Woooonderful!" Joan gushed. She grasped Alexa's hand to draw her away. "Do you mind if I borrow her?"

"Only for a moment," Leonardo chided.

"I haven't seen her in so long, I need to catch up." Joan then carted Alexa off to a corner of the room. She grabbed two glasses of wine and handed one to Alexa before they both sat down in two thick-cushioned armchairs with a small table between them.

"How've you been, darlin'?" she asked finally, taking a sip of the fine wine. Her well-manicured fingers were covered in jewels.

"Well, I've been really busy the past few months." Although she and Joan were friends, Alexa wasn't sure what she should and shouldn't say. Considering she would be out of Leonardo's life in a couple of months, she almost felt guilty at the pleasure their reconciliation gave to Joan.

"Busy, huh?" Joan looked at her out of the corner of her eye while keeping her gaze trained on her guests circulating in the room. "That's good to hear, I suppose. If I were you, I would have been falling apart over missing that fine specimen of a husband you have there."

Alexa shifted, unsure of the direction in which Joan was taking the conversation. "I did miss him," she admitted, which was the truth.

"I know you did." Joan nodded her head and placed her glass on the table. Resting her elbow on the arm of the chair, she leaned toward Alexa. "He missed you something awful, too. I tell you what, whatever happened to make the two of you separate, I hope it never happens again. That poor man looked like death warmed over right after you left."

This was news to Alexa. Joan was implying that Leonardo had missed her and their separation had been difficult for him.

"Death warmed over?"

"Mhmm." Joan waved a greeting at someone nearby. "I wanted to call you, but I didn't know if you'd even take my call. Russell and I were friends with Leonardo first, and since y'all were no longer together, I assumed that you had washed your hands of his friends, as well."

"No, nothing could be further from truth!" Alexa reached out and touched her friend's arm. "To be honest with you, Joan, I missed you. I wanted to call, but like you, I wasn't sure if I would be welcome to contact you since you were Leo's friends first."

"Well, isn't that something?" Joan laughed, squeezing Alexa's hand between her own. "You never have to worry about calling me, darlin'. I'm always available." Joan picked up her glass again and took another sip. "Oh, before I forget, I've got some things for The Closet I think you'll love. I was going to give them to another charity, but I'd rather you have them. I can have them brought down to the store in a couple of days."

"That would be wonderful, but we have a van available for large donations if that would be more convenient."

"Oh, no, I won't hear of it. It'll give our driver an assignment that doesn't include us so he can take care of some personal errands. He likes getting a break from us once in a while." She winked.

"Thank you so much, Joan. Your donation will make a lot of women so happy."

"Don't thank me yet, until you see the loot." Joan sucked in her stomach with a deep breath, and then she let it out with a huge whoosh. "I've done lost my girlish figure, and there may not be that many women who can benefit from clothes that size."

Alexa thought Joan was being too hard on herself. She was certainly not fat, and her womanly figure was appropriate for a healthy woman in her late fifties. "I'm sure Russell's not complaining, so I wouldn't worry about it."

Joan had the grace to blush. "Well, I suppose you're right."

"Congratulations, Joan," a woman said, stopping to plant an air kiss near Joan's cheek. "I hope the two of you have thirty more years together!"

Alexa almost choked on her wine when she recognized the red hair. Her hair was in an updo tonight, but it was definitely the woman she had seen outside the restaurant with Leonardo.

"Thank you, darlin.'"

"Who was that?" Alexa croaked when the other woman floated away.

"Oh, that's one of the attorneys in Russell's firm. Smart girl." A look of embarrassment came over her face. "Smart as a whip, but I can't for the life of me remember her name. Russell assigned her as the lead attorney on the Latin American expansion."

Alexa felt the tension drain from her body. At least there was a reasonable explanation for why Leonardo had been with the other woman. They really had been working. She vaguely remembered Leonardo working on the deals to enter the markets in Central and South America.

"Oh no," Alexa heard the older woman groan.

She turned a questioning eye in the direction Joan was looking. Russell was signaling to Joan near a table piled high with heavy hors d'oeuvres.

"What is it?"

"He wants to make a toast, and of course that means one of his so-called funny stories about our married life." She made a dramatic roll of her eyes.

Alexa smiled to herself. Although Joan acted as if she were embarrassed and annoyed by her husband's anecdotal tales, she also knew how much Joan loved him and thought the world of him. Their marriage was rock solid despite their differences, and to the amusement of friends, they often bantered back and forth, giving each other a hard time.

Joan rose from the chair, but before she walked away, she said, "We need to get together for lunch one day to catch up. And definitely before that husband of yours whisks you away in two months to spend the next three years in Brazil."

Alexa's hand with the glass froze halfway to her mouth. "The next three years?"

"Yes. While he's setting up the Latin American headquarters for Radiant Communications, darlin'," Joan said matter-of-factly, as if it were common knowledge. Perhaps it was, but this tidbit of information was news to Alexa.

As Joan hurried away, Alexa scanned the room in search of Leonardo.

Leonardo was moving to Brazil for three years?

The sound of a metal fork clinking against glass drew Alexa's attention to the center of the room, where Joan was standing, staring up adoringly at her husband. All conversations ceased, and the guests faced the couple celebrating another year of their happy marriage.

Russell Simpson lapsed into one of his stories, and Alexa half listened as she pondered what Joan had said. Leonardo was leaving for Brazil in two months. Sixty days.

A round of applause shook her from her ruminations and forced her to concentrate her attention on the celebration taking place in the room. She saw Joan bent back across Russell's arm as he planted a passionate kiss on her lips. The romantic gesture made Alexa feel a twinge of jealousy, wishing she and Leonardo could have reached the thirty-year milestone in their marriage and share the kind of love Russell and Joan did.

She started. What was she thinking? She and Leonardo couldn't share that type of relationship because their marriage was doomed almost from the beginning and was over even now. The excitement of being married to a powerful, rich, sexy man waned under the reality of day-to-day life.

He was no longer charming and playful. With work consuming all his time, her role became one of hostess and bed partner. There was nothing in between. The times she spent alone were a constant reminder of the mockery of a marriage she saw between her parents, and she had been determined she wouldn't repeat the same mistakes.

The guests began to mill about again when the kiss ended. Alexa lifted her glass from the table to take another swallow before getting to her feet.

Intuitively, she sensed Leonardo's gaze on her, and she caught sight of him near the entrance to the balcony. He was watching her, though he should have been engrossed in the conversation with the two other people with whom he was standing, one of which was the redhead. Even from that distance across the room, she could sense his desire for her, and there was an answering pounding of the blood in her veins as their gazes locked.

Maybe it was the kiss between Russell and Joan and the romantic notion of long-lasting love, but Alexa found her thoughts straying to memories of sharing passionate kisses with Leonardo. She carefully placed her glass of wine on the table before it slipped from her damp fingers and crashed onto the expensive white carpet. She felt nervous and jittery because she knew the reason for Leonardo's smoldering scrutiny. She was fully aware what was expected of her, and she found herself breathlessly anticipating the end of the evening.

Leonardo came toward her, his lithe, graceful walk a surprise for a man of his size. The tuxedo jacket hugged his broad shoulders and fit his muscular frame like a glove. As he neared her, Alexa realized she was holding her breath. The undercurrent of sexual tension flared between them.

"Are you nervous?" Leonardo asked.

"Why would I be nervous?" Her voice came out breathy, husky. She cleared her throat.

Leonardo smiled knowingly. He must feel the same charge, know that she longed to be kissed and touched, despite being coerced into resuming her role as his wife.

He didn't answer her question. "You haven't eaten a thing all night."

It was true, but how could he possibly know that? She didn't have an appetite for much except the tall, dark man standing before her.

"I've had my eye on you all evening," he said in response to the unspoken question.

The thought that he'd been watching her even during the periods when they were separated generated tiny little shivers across Alexa's skin. Her fingers tightened around the clutch in her left hand. "I'm not hungry."

The knowing smile widened. "You should eat something," he said. His dark gaze lingered in appreciation on the split in her dress. "You're going to need your energy."

CHAPTER 6

*A*lexa's heart surged, slamming against her breastbone. There was no way her willpower could withstand the thump levied by his innuendo.

"So it's tonight, then?" she asked unnecessarily.

"Was there ever any doubt?" Leonardo countered. His predatory smile left no room for ambiguity regarding his intentions.

"No. Not where you're concerned."

He lifted his hand and let his forefinger trace down the length of her narrow face. "Have I told you how beautiful you look tonight?" he asked, his voice low and filled with warmth.

Alexa shook her head, emotion piled high in her throat so that she couldn't speak. It was difficult to resist him when he was so charming. It was one of the things that had made her fall so fast and hard in love with him. He could turn it on whenever he chose, and his charm was lethal, able to slice through her inadequate objections.

"You are very beautiful tonight, *querida*."

He leaned forward. There was only the slightest brush of his lips across hers, yet the featherlight touch evoked an explosive response. Alexa felt her stomach muscles contract painfully, and her breath caught in her throat. She wanted him, and when he pulled back, there was no doubt he could see the truth in her eyes.

"We should leave now," Leonardo stated.

"We've barely been here an hour. What will people think?"

"When have you ever known me to care what people think?"

It was true. Leonardo da Silva didn't concern himself with social norms. He wasn't one to inconvenience himself at the expense of others. If someone else had a problem with something he did, it was their problem, not his. For him it was enough that he had come out in support of his friends' celebration. He was ready to leave, so he would.

He took Alexa's arm just below the elbow and started moving toward the door.

Like a hot-blooded robot, she remained in step with him. Her body was responding to the proximity of his, his masculine scent, and the warmth of the long, firm fingers lightly pressed against the tender flesh of her arm.

It wasn't hard to understand why she still wanted him so much, but she didn't want to be so easy. She wanted to be tough and make it difficult for him to seduce her back between the sheets. Instead, it was glaringly clear he would not find seduction was necessary at all, because she was ready and willing to succumb to any of his demands.

On the way to the door, they said their good-byes to the hosts. The Simpsons expressed their disappointment that they were leaving so soon, but also their pleasure that the two had found their way back together. After a bit more small talk, they departed.

The Porsche ate up the miles of Highway 85, a main thoroughfare that ran through the heart of Atlanta and its surrounding counties. At first, neither one of them broke the silence in the car as they barreled toward home. The chemistry was still just as strong between them, and the pulsing ache in Alexa's body increased the longer they were in the car.

In the four months since they'd separated, she hadn't thought of anyone else, hadn't even considered becoming intimate with another man. There was no point in pretending any other man could make her feel this way, because it had always only been Leonardo. The maleness of him, the temptation to feel him hard, pressed between her thighs, was unbearable. She needed to quiet her heated thoughts, which included the very dangerous idea of climbing onto his lap to straddle him while he drove.

"Leo?"

What was it she wanted to say? Could she adequately express what she was feeling? She was afraid of the force of her emotions, and she was concerned their short reconciliation would leave her even more scarred, more broken than after their separation.

"What is it, Alexa?" he asked when she didn't continue.

Could she tell him? Could she admit what she'd only just come to terms with herself—that she loved her husband, had never stopped loving him, and wished they were back together permanently?

"Do you hate me for what I did?" she asked quietly. "For leaving you?"

He glanced over at her before his eyes resumed looking through the windshield. The lights from an oncoming vehicle swept across his taut features, the well-defined square jaw, the high cheekbones.

"I don't hate you, Alexa, and I never did."

She let out a relieved breath. "But you want to punish me."

"I did," Leonardo admitted. "I was angry at you. You left with little explanation, except a short voice mail that didn't really tell me anything I needed to know. So yes, I wanted to punish you at one time, but that's no longer of interest to me." He glanced at her again. "I don't want you to be concerned about what's going to happen tonight. I do want to make love to you, but you have to want this, too. I would never force myself on you. Do you want this, Alexa? Or do you see it as a punishment—something you have to suffer through?"

There was no need to define what "this" was. "This" was almost a tangible life force between them. "This" was propelling them forward with the promise of bliss, yet they were entering the unknown because of the amount of time that had passed since they were last together.

"No, it's not a punishment, Leo. I want this. I want you. I want to make love to you." Her voice trembled with need. "I can't wait."

He reached for her, then squeezed her slender fingers in his hand. His hold was tight, too tight, but she didn't protest. She understood his reaction, because the same strong, almost violent feelings gnawed at her insides.

He held on to her all the way back to the house. Once inside the gates, the car slowed to a stop in front of the large front door of their home.

He brought her hand to his mouth and pressed his lips against her knuckles. The warmth of anticipation spread across her abdomen. "Go upstairs. I'll be right in to join you."

LEONARDO WATCHED as Alexa exited the vehicle. The clinging green dress was the perfect complement to her honey-colored skin and left little to the imagination. It had tantalized him all night, and he'd been in a tortured semierect state since they left the house.

Once the door was closed behind her, he faced forward and intended to drive around the side to place the car in the multi-vehicle garage. Instead, he didn't move and turned off the ignition. All he could think about was that he had his wife back. It was finally sinking in.

It had been the longest four months of his life. He should have chased after her, put himself out of his misery. Instead, he allowed his pride to keep him away, and he'd suffered the consequences of his stubbornness. He hadn't had a good night's sleep since she left. He walked around like an automaton because, even when he was exhausted, he only managed to get in a few hours of fitful rest at a time.

Having his marriage crumble around him had been difficult to endure, and Leonardo was still hard pressed to fully understand what had really gone wrong. Yes, he and Alexa had some differences, but how they'd managed to morph into an insurmountable roadblock on their journey through married life had taken him by surprise.

In hindsight, he realized the signs had been there for several months, but he'd ignored them and continued working on the plans for the Latin American expansion that were consuming his every waking moment. Then one day he returned home, and before he even listened to the message, the eerie emptiness of their bedroom suite had portended her absence.

Leonardo unfolded his tall frame from the car and slammed the door. As always, he forced himself into the present, refusing to languish in the regrets of the past. He made a decision then. It was a decision he hadn't expected would come forth when he originally hatched his plan to get Alexa back.

Originally, all he thought he wanted was to get revenge for the heartless way she had abandoned their marriage. He relished the thought of bending her to his will, and he couldn't wait to have what he'd lost, enjoy what he'd been denied for four long months. His breathing was ragged as he recollected the pleasure of her full lips pliant against his. Or better yet, having her sucking and pulling on him until he lost his sanity and exploded into her soft, sweet mouth.

The keys Leonardo held scored across his palm as he squeezed them in his hand. He was getting harder by the second.

The truth was, he'd fooled himself into thinking he wanted revenge. He had been angry when she left, but that wasn't why he'd ultimately made his indecent proposal to her. It was because he'd missed her. She'd made his house into a home. Just knowing she was there, night after night, no matter how late he worked, brought him peace. When he lowered his tired body into bed next to her late at night, it comforted him to have the sound of her gentle breathing lull him to sleep.

Yes, he'd made his decision. It was very simple. Unlike his parents' marriage, his would not end in divorce.

* * *

ALEXA STOOD JUST inside the door, unable to move. She'd turned on the light to ensure she didn't stumble as she made her way up the stairs, but neither of her feet had landed on a single stair.

She was torn. Part of her wanted to rush up the stairs, another part of her felt a nervous excitement like it was the first time with Leonardo all over again, and a third part wanted to wait for him. She didn't want to climb the stairs alone.

The decision to go up or stay downstairs was taken out of her hands when the door opened and closed behind her. She spun around. He should have come through the kitchen, not the front door.

"Did you put away the car?" she asked in a breathy voice. She didn't really care about the car.

"No," Leonardo replied.

"But you always put the Porsche in the garage." She was babbling, nervous energy loosening her lips into unnecessary discourse.

His hot gaze rested on her. With long strides, he closed the gap between them. "I didn't want to waste another second, when I could be doing this instead."

He hauled her to him, lowering his lips to hers and enfolding her in his arms. Raw need bolted through them.

Her clutch fell from her nerveless fingers as he pushed his tongue into her mouth and crushed her closer against his hard frame. This was what she wanted, had ached for in the close confines of the car. Alexa leaned into him, her mouth softening and widening to allow his tongue access to stroke and prod at will.

Leonardo's right hand inched up her bare thigh, while the fingers of his left hand spread across her breasts, squeezing and kneading the soft mounds in turn until she gasped into his mouth. Her nipples swelled and hardened, pressing against the barrier of the dress, threatening to break free of the silk.

Still he deepened the kiss, angling his head so he could hungrily devour her mouth, pressing her back against the wall of the foyer.

"Touch me, Alexa," he groaned. "Please."

Eager to please, Alexa slid her hands down the front of his shirt in an agonizingly slow crawl, his contoured chest expanding as she became reacquainted with the magnificent body beneath the material. The belt on his trousers was no match for her nimble fingers, and when she took his length in her hands, his body was gripped with shudders, a groan of agony leaving him and finding an answering shiver deep inside her, rocking her to the core.

She stroked his hard flesh with expert familiarity, exulted by the fact that she could have control over such a powerful man. He groaned again when she picked up the pace of her strokes, the throbbing heat of his member a welcome reminder of what was to come. She wanted him so much she thought for sure she would soon burst into flames from the heat of her own lust.

With shaky fingers, Leonardo grasped her hands and

removed them from his body and pinned her between his hips and the cool surface behind her. He brought his mouth down on hers again with a deep-seated hunger, his tongue wrestling and dancing with hers in a sexy samba.

"Leo," she whispered when he released her mouth, only to drop a trail of fire with his tongue across her neck.

Her arms locked around his neck when he picked her up from the floor and walked into the library.

There was no way they could make it up the stairs, and it was the nearest room. A lamp gave enough light for him to find his way over to the sofa and lower her onto her back.

The gold clasp on her shoulder was undone with speedy efficacy, and the top half of her dress was pulled down to expose her abundant breasts to his ravenous gaze.

"Beautiful," he murmured in appreciation, just before he lifted her into his hungry mouth.

Alexa's shoulders jerked back, she cried out, and her body bowed beneath him. She panted as she struggled to catch her breath, delighting in the torture he inflicted on her heated flesh as his mouth and tongue worried the hard, caramel-colored tip of her left breast.

She was reeling out of control, every muscle taut and aching for the relaxation that would come once their bodies were joined. She stroked her fingers through the hair at his collar, then tunneled higher with a massaging motion across his scalp. "Leo, Leo . . ."

His relentless mouth fastened onto the other breast, sucking and pulling as she squirmed helplessly beneath him. Meanwhile, one hand stroked across the damp satin barrier that covered the most sensitive part of her body. Electrifying tingles suffused every inch of her body as he boldly stroked and caressed her between her legs, kissed and licked greedily at her breasts.

"It's been so long," Leonardo said, his accent so thick his voice was barely recognizable. "I need to be inside you, *querida*."

When he shifted his body to remove her panties, her stomach muscles quivered in excitement. Then he was poised over her, resting his body on his elbows as he gazed down into her upturned face.

"This is where you belong." His right knee nudged her legs apart, and his hips moved with a possessive thrust to join them together.

Alexa lifted her body up to meet his, locking her arms around his neck. He shoved his fingers into her hair, grabbing a fistful of the sleek dark strands to yank her head back so he could scrape his teeth along her arched throat.

She loved it, the way he took control of her, the way he took control of everything. Her body strained to get even closer to him. She trembled in his arms and wrapped her legs tightly around his waist, lifting her heels higher along his back so she could take him deeper.

In their feverish craze, they hadn't even bothered to remove their clothes. Her elegant green gown was crumpled around her waist, while his boxers and tuxedo pants were pushed just low enough to allow him the ease with which to penetrate her. It was uncivilized, primal.

His heavy grunts intermingled with her tortured moans while they moved together as one. Nothing else mattered at the moment—not the misunderstandings, not the pain of the past, only the synchronized rhythm of each advance and retreat of his hard flesh into the moist heat of her body in the race toward fulfillment.

Before long, the pending tension built up inside Alexa, her breath coming in short spurts. He knew her too well. He knew just the right spot, and he hit it over and over with swift but controlled drives until she cried out her release.

She felt weightless, as if she were floating above herself, her untethered body spasming as the world tilted dangerously off-kilter. Leonardo could no longer contain himself once she contracted around him. He was no longer in control as he pumped faster into her. Finally, he loudly grunted his own release, his warm breath whispering across her collarbone as he emptied himself inside her.

Moments later, Alexa lay in a daze, shaken by the power of her climax. She was half on top of Leonardo, his right hand placed loosely around her waist while his left dragged against the floor. Her dress had been pulled down to modestly cover her exposed bottom, but he'd refused to allow her to pull up the bodice of the dress to cover her breasts. His pants were pulled up, though not closed.

Alexa shut her eyes, her languid body relaxed and contented.

CHAPTER 7

*O*nce in their bedroom, they removed all their clothing and made love again in a slower, exploratory fashion. Alexa was now cradled in Leonardo's arms under the cream-colored sheets, her back flush against his hair-roughened chest. The curtains were drawn open so they could look out at the full moon and the inky black of the star-splattered sky. Their tawny limbs were intertwined, and his hand stroked in a soothing motion from her knee to her hip.

Alexa hesitated to broach the topic she had shelved away in preference to enjoying the pleasure of being made love to by Leonardo. Nevertheless, she wanted to press him for answers about the growth into the Latin American markets.

She stilled the movement of his hand by covering it with her own. "Joan mentioned something tonight I want to ask you about. What she said took me by surprise, and I want to know if it's true."

"What is it?"

"She said you'll be moving to Brazil for three years. Is that true?"

When there was no answer, Alexa twisted around in his

arms. Their faces almost touched they were so close, but she couldn't tell what he was thinking. His eyes were shuttered, effectively hiding his innermost thoughts.

"I've thought about it."

The brief answer was unexpected. After the intimacies they just shared, she had hoped he would be more forthcoming and provide details about his plans. Deep down, she'd harbored the secret hope he was about to make changes that would affect their future—creating an opportunity for them to have a better relationship.

"And if you leave, you'll leave in two months?"

A speculative look came over Leonardo's face. He eased his arm from beneath Alexa and propped his head in his palm so he could look down at her as she lay nestled against the fluffy pillows. "Why are you suddenly so interested in my business affairs? As I recall, there was never any interest before."

"I'm just curious. It came as a surprise to me that you planned to move to Brazil for such a long time. I know how important the company is to you, and I was surprised that you planned to leave the U.S. headquarters to spend so much time in Brazil." Important was an understatement. Radiant Communications was his oxygen. Sixteen-hour work days had made that clear enough.

"The company is important to me." He paused before continuing. "My father inherited Radiant Communications when he was a young man. Through my contributions, the firm has grown in size and revenue, and I'm proud of everything I and my team have accomplished. I decided to take the lead in Brazil because I understand the culture and feel comfortable leaving the company in the hands of some of the executives and a few family members. I'll also enjoy the slower pace in Brazil."

"Is it really possible for you to slow down?" Alexa asked.

"I already have." He looked affronted, frowning down at her

as if she'd insulted him. "As I showed you earlier today, I can leave work early."

"And what caused this change?"

The intensity of Leonardo's stare increased, and he lifted his thumb to trace along the line of her delicate jaw to her chin. "In my old age," he began with a cynical smile, "I've realized there are more important things than work."

Breathing momentarily suspended, Alexa lowered her lids immediately to hide the feelings charging through her. She didn't want to get her hopes up, but it certainly seemed possible their marriage could take on a new life. She was willing to take the plunge, to believe he was talking about their marriage, but she was unsure whether or not his mindset was the same as hers. To reconcile and wake up next to him every day would make the torment of the last four months worth it.

He traced the same finger over the curve of her full lower lip.

She lifted her gaze to him. How she loved this man!

Could they start over? Would he invite her to Brazil after the period of their arrangement had expired?

"What are you thinking right now?" Leonardo asked, lowering his head so that his lips were mere millimeters away from hers.

He was in seduction mode again, which was fine with Alexa. She figured she'd learned all she could because she was now distracted by the mouth that hovered temptingly above her. The erotic memory of their frantic coupling in the library and then the sensuous manner in which their bodies came together in bed made her heartbeat pick up speed. With Leonardo's tender touch, her body was coming back alive, and hope fluttered in her chest.

"I was thinking about how much I want you," she whispered seductively, lowering her lids so her lashes almost brushed against her cheeks.

There was a rumble in Leonardo's chest as he quickly settled himself over her.

* * *

THE NEXT MORNING, Alexa slowly opened her eyes to find herself alone in the bed. She was mildly disappointed because she expected to wake up in Leonardo's arms. She had gravitated to his side of the bed, like she always did. Her cheek rested on the pillow his head previously occupied. She closed her eyes briefly and inhaled sharply to get a good whiff of the woodsy scent of his cologne and his intoxicating maleness. She smiled, laughing at herself. She was behaving like a woman in love, and she couldn't wait to see the object of her affection.

Stretching, Alexa turned over and saw he had closed the curtains so the sunlight wouldn't come in and awaken her too early. She smiled to herself again. It was Saturday. Maybe they could do something together today. She dared hope, even though she knew she risked disappointment. She felt optimistic after the passionate night they shared, and her wishful thinking propelled her from the bed.

After taking a quick shower, she moisturized her body with a flowery-scented lotion and then threw on a white silk robe. She took her time going down the stairs. The house was quieter than usual because most of the servants had the weekend off. Only a small staff reported on the weekend, and they remained largely unseen unless called for.

Since Leonardo's office was on the ground floor, she searched for him there first.

Knocking lightly on the oak wood door, she waited to hear a response, but there was no answer. She tried the doorknob, found it to be unlocked, and entered.

"Leo?" she called uncertainly.

Alexa peered around the office. It was similar in design to

his office at the Radiant Communications building. The design was minimalist, with glass and leather furniture dominating the decor. This office had French doors that opened onto an outdoor patio, and there was a wall of shelves that contained numerous business books and knickknacks from Brazil.

Thinking Leonardo must be in some other part of the house, Alexa was about to walk out when she heard his muffled voice just beyond the French doors. They were cracked open about an inch, and when she walked over, she saw him standing with his back to the house. He held his cell phone to his ear and was engaged in what must clearly be a very intense conversation.

Unlike her, he was fully dressed, looking comfortable in a faded blue T-shirt that hung loosely on his broad chest. His worn blue jeans hugged his lean hips and encased his powerful, muscular thighs. He walked slowly back and forth, a clear indication of irritation etched in his profile.

Thinking it was best to leave him alone, Alexa would have walked out except a folder on his desk caught her eye. The manila folder was partially hidden beneath a stack of blue folders, but the undercut was clearly showing. The handwritten label had "Xander Dixon" written on it. She hesitated. Why would Leonardo have a Xander file on his desk?

Moving quietly, Alexa inched closer and slipped the folder from beneath the stack. She realized she was prying, but how could she not when it clearly involved her brother somehow?

Heat rushed through Alexa's body when she opened the folder and scanned the contents. Enclosed was a memo to one of the portfolio managers of Atlanta Finance Corporation from Leonardo, in his position as president of the board of directors. AFC held Xander's loan!

Alexa gulped as she read the instructions. To her utmost dismay, his instructions were to exercise the clause in Xander's loan. She flipped through the additional pages, which included a full copy of Xander's loan, supporting documents, and an e-mail from the portfolio manager notifying Leonardo he had done as asked.

It was all clear now. The fact that AFC was enforcing the clause so quickly after Xander had missed his payments was always a surprise to her, but now it made sense. Leonardo had his hand in it, and the reason was clear. She thought he'd helped Xander, but instead he'd been punishing him because of her, and in order to get back at her. Then she'd gone to him. Like a fly, she'd flown straight into his spider's web. All he had to do was wait for her to show up, and then he could get his revenge.

Blazing fury took over at that moment. She would never forgive him for this. Leonardo was ruthless and unfeeling, and now she could add unethical to the list of disparaging adjectives reserved just for him.

"What are you doing?"

Alexa swung in the direction of Leonardo's voice. He stood just inside the French doors. He looked like he knew exactly what she was doing, and by his furrowed brow, he wasn't pleased. Well, neither was she.

"I can't believe you!" she spat. "You knew all along. You knew Xander was in financial trouble because you set it in motion!"

Leonardo fixated on the folder in Alexa's hand, and she itched to toss it and the contents in his arrogant face.

"You should never snoop in someone else's things," he said coolly, taking his time to walk over to the desk. He placed his cell phone on top of it. "Especially when it's none of your business."

"None of my business?" Alexa all but screeched. She slammed the folder onto the desk. "This most definitely is my business because I'm here as a direct result of what you did. You used your influence on the board to have the portfolio manager accelerate the payment on my brother's loan, and you used that to blackmail me into coming back here and faking a reconciliation with you."

"You were never blackmailed," Leonardo said between gritted teeth. He leaned forward on the palms of his hands. "You had a choice, and you made it. I never forced you back here."

Alexa laughed. It was a hollow sound. "You actually believe that, don't you? In your twisted mind, I *chose* to come back here. Never mind that I practically begged you for an alternative so I wouldn't have to." She shook with anger. "So, did you get your revenge? Are you satisfied? Did you get your pound of flesh?"

Leonardo straightened, dragging his gaze down her slender body covered in the robe. Self-consciously, she tightened the belt knot, pulling the garment closer against her body.

A ghost of a smile hovered at the corner of his lips. "We have an agreement, remember? I haven't come close to getting all the flesh I want."

Alexa's treacherous body pulsed to life. Her weakness for him was annoying. "That agreement is null and void. There's no way I'm sleeping with you again."

He looked unconcerned by her declaration. In fact, he looked amused, which only served to infuriate her further. "Do you really want to play this game, Alexa? Because we both know who will win."

"I'm not playing a game. You should have gotten a contract like I suggested. What choice do you have if I walk out the front door? You've already given the money to Xander, so you have no leverage."

Leonardo made his way around the desk. Alexa kept her distance by taking a step back.

"On the contrary, I do have leverage. A check of that amount will be held by the bank for at least three days. Therefore . . ." He let his voice trail off dramatically, adding an elegant shrug.

Alexa never considered that, and too late she realized she'd spoken too soon. "You can't withhold that money. I've already given it to him, and he believes it's his. He was so happy because his problems were solved."

"I did give it to him, with certain conditions." Leonardo sat on the edge of the desk and did his signature move of crossing his arms over his chest. "But as of this conversation—what you just said—the terms have changed, so I don't see any reason why he should still get that money."

"You're the reason he needed it in the first place!" Alexa said in exasperation.

"*Xander* is the reason," Leonardo said firmly. "Don't pretend with me, and don't let your loyalty to your brother cloud your judgment. He's a great baker, but you're the one who took after your father when it comes to running a business. What I did was for his own good and gave him a wake-up call. You know as well as I do that Xander is incapable of managing his business affairs."

"You could have cut him a break. You could have used your influence to help him instead of hurt him." Alexa shook her head slowly. "But we both know why you did that. You wanted to get back at me."

"I don't usually give orgasms to people I'm trying to get back at," Leonardo said dryly.

Alexa straightened her spine, even more irritated by his comments. "Is that what all of this is to you—a big joke?"

Leonardo sobered. "There's nothing funny about this situation. Your brother needed to be taught a lesson in business. He had two hundred and fifty thousand dollars of the bank's money, and he was mismanaging it, like he always does. You would have swooped in and taken care of the situation for him before too long, and then he wouldn't have learned anything or grown as a business owner. Now, he's debt free—he doesn't owe the finance company a dime. He's also learned a valuable lesson, and I'm sure once he gets the office manager in place, he'll be even better off."

"So you've done your good deed for the year?" Alexa asked snidely. "I don't for one second believe you did that for the good of my brother."

"As you well know, I wasn't being completely altruistic." He let his heated gaze run over her body once more. "I did get something out of it." When he lifted his eyes to hers, she could see the dilation of the pupils, a clear indication he was aroused.

"Me." There was no need for confirmation.

To her shame, Alexa felt the answering heat in her body. Even her anger couldn't prevent her from wanting him. She'd wanted him and wanted to be near him, so that was why she'd searched out his company earlier, only to uncover the ghastly truth that had brought her back into his life.

"So now we're at a standoff," Leonardo said softly. "You have another decision to make. Do you still want to walk away, or do you stay and finish out the terms we agreed on?"

All her foolish, optimistic hopes and dreams were smashed against the rocks of reality. Leonardo set it all up to get back at her and teach her brother a lesson. He was certainly determined to teach the siblings a lesson, according to his own educational policies.

It was time Leonardo was taught a lesson. He needed to learn the end didn't justify the means, and he would no longer be able to coerce her into continuing her "wifely duties."

"This time I'll make the right choice." She wished she could hide the tremor in her voice. "I'm leaving, Leo. Xander and I will figure something out about the money."

An indefinable emotion flitted across his face. It was a combination of surprise and something else she couldn't decipher.

"You're not leaving," he said, his tone hard, brooking no argument.

"What are you going to do? Tie me up and force me to stay here?"

His eyes lit up at the offhand question, and Alexa suddenly remembered their honeymoon in Paris and how he'd bound her to the bed. It was the one and only time they'd done it, but it had been insanely pleasurable.

She suddenly found it difficult to breathe, her chest moving up and down quickly as she fought to get more oxygen.

"Is that what you want, Alexa?" He shifted to stand upright. "Do you want me to tie you up and force you to stay?"

Yes. Because she would enjoy it. Because then she could blame him for what they would do the moment he put his hands on her.

"No," Alexa said instead. "What I want is for you to leave me alone. I don't . . ." She couldn't say it. She couldn't deny wanting him. It was such a blatant lie.

"Do you know what I want?" Leonardo asked in a lowered voice, taking a step toward her. She didn't move, afraid if she did her legs wouldn't support her. "I want you to stay." He took another step forward, and now he was standing directly in front of her, looking down at her, all six feet three inches of magnificent male. "I want to put my fingers between your thighs and see if you're already moist for me."

She wished he wouldn't say such things. It made her nipples perk up and chafe against the robe.

"It's over," she insisted with difficulty.

"No, it's not. I set the terms."

Her knees almost buckled when she took two steps back. He took two forward. Seconds later, one hair-sprinkled arm whipped out and grasped the nape of her neck. His head descended toward hers, and his tongue plundered its way into the warm recesses of her mouth.

She held back for as long as she could, fisting her hands against his chest in the closest act to rebellion she could muster, even while her lips clung to his like a lifeline. His large hand easily pushed aside the robe to uncover the curly hairs between her hips. He'd barely touched her, but she was spreading her legs to accommodate him.

"Just as I suspected," he murmured hoarsely when he discovered the evidence of her desire. He stroked across her damp, swollen flesh, lighting a fire deep within her that threatened to burn out of control. She sank her teeth into the flesh of her inner lip to resist the urge to moan aloud. "What are we going to do about this now?"

Alexa sunk her nails into his wide shoulders. "Stop torturing me."

His grin was one of satisfaction. "Whatever you want."

Lifting Alexa up into his arms, Leonardo exited the office, and they were through the doors of the bedroom so fast he must have taken the stairs two at a time. They disrobed quickly, kissing and nipping at each other as each inch of flesh was exposed.

But Leonardo had plans for her. He lifted the belt of the silk robe from the floor and held it aloft for her to see. "I want to make sure you don't go anywhere."

As if she would leave now, knowing what was so close. Anticipation licked at her spine, and heat warmed her inner thighs when Leonardo bound each wrist to the cool iron bars of the bed. He was focused, resolute, testing each knot before he began his attack.

Everywhere his hands went, his mouth followed: across her swollen breasts, skimming the sensitive flesh of her abdomen, lingering at the damp juncture between her thighs. Tied as she was to the bed, she could do nothing except accept the invasive thrust of his tongue and fingers between her legs.

His assault on her was merciless, but all she could do was whimper and writhe against him, because he refused to untie her. Her begging was in vain. She tugged on the belt, but it was an exercise in futility. He would keep her there as long as he wanted, and she wouldn't be released until he was finished.

CHAPTER 8

*L*ater in the day, after dusk fell on the city, Leonardo stood bare-chested and barefoot on the balcony outside the bedroom. He'd slipped back into his jeans after easing out of bed so as not to disturb Alexa, who was fast asleep.

They'd made love several times and then fallen into exhausted sleep. Upon awakening, he'd requested a late lunch be brought up to their room, and then they'd drifted into sleep again.

He stared, unseeing, into the pool of water below him. He still craved her. She was like a drug—the only drug that could assuage the painful throbbing in his groin.

The last thing he ever expected was that she would call his bluff about Xander. When he set his plan in motion, he knew he was taking a risk. It was quite possible she and Xander could have found someone else to help them, but he betted against the odds. What did he have to lose? If Plan A didn't work, then he would simply have to create a Plan B.

It worked, but not for long. She was furious now she knew he influenced the decision to demand the full amount of the loan. His plan had backfired, and it was rare Leonardo found himself in a predicament where all the loose ends didn't tie up neatly. Yet here he was.

There was only one way to handle this, but he was concerned about the response he would get. Deep down, Leonardo knew the right thing to do was to allow her the option to go. Even though they made love as if they could never get enough of each other, that wasn't enough, either. She had to *want* to stay.

If she didn't want to stay, he would have no choice but to let her go—again. He shut his eyes as the worst pain he could ever imagine suffused him.

* * *

FOR THE SECOND time that day, Alexa awoke to find herself alone in bed. Only this time, the person she searched for was standing at the foot of the bed, watching her. When her eyes met his, however, his face became shuttered, as if he quickly rearranged his features to hide something.

"Did you get enough sleep?" Leonardo asked.

The darkening day amplified the husky intimacy of his voice. He was breathtaking in just his jeans. The silken hairs on his chest arrowed down below his waistband, toward the part of his body she'd thoroughly enjoyed three times today.

Alexa nodded and then swallowed. Despite looking irresistible, she couldn't miss that he also appeared very somber. He must have something very serious weighing on his mind.

"We need to talk about us," Leonardo said.

Alexa sat up slowly, tucking the sheet under her arms. She ran her fingers over her rumpled hair. He had her undivided attention, and hope leapt in her chest. "What about us?"

"We can't continue like this. Every time we fight, we end up in bed."

Alexa cleared her throat. "And whose fault is that?"

"I would have to say both our faults, since you don't give any indication you want me to stop. Unless I've misread the signs?"

He knew good and well he hadn't misread the signs. She was an enthusiastic participant.

"No, you haven't," she admitted.

Leonardo nodded before continuing. "We don't resolve our problems. We need to address them head-on."

Alexa held her tongue. She didn't want to comment until she understood his direction. Did he think they needed marriage counseling, maybe? Whatever it took to get them back on track, she was willing. If salvaging their marriage was a priority for him, it certainly was for her.

"We haven't addressed our problems," he continued, "and of course, I've been somewhat of a bully. Therefore, I've decided to change the terms of our arrangement. You may leave. I have no right to keep you here."

"What are you saying?" She spoke so lowly she could barely hear herself. It was a wonder he even heard her. Rubber band-like tension squeezed her heart relentlessly, making it difficult to think. Her brain was frozen, in shock. Hours before he'd insisted she could not leave until he was ready, until the terms of their arrangement were concluded. Now, he was more or less kicking her out.

His jaw tensed noticeably. "I'm saying you're free to go—if that's what you want."

Free to go. That *had* been what she wanted, but now . . . Now she was calmer, she was back to wanting to stay.

"What about Xander and the . . . money?" Alexa couldn't look at him anymore. Her gaze settled on the cream-colored sheets, and she began to pluck at nonexistent loose threads. She couldn't bear for him to see the pain in her eyes.

"The money is his."

There it was. She no longer could use the excuse that he'd forced her to come here, because it was an excuse. Even though consciously she rebelled against the idea of returning as Leonardo's wife, she now had to admit that on a subconscious level, she'd missed him, their lovemaking, and their friends, and her life hadn't been the same. Without him, her life was empty, barren. Now he was relegating her back to that paltry existence, and just the thought of it made her want to sob out loud.

Alexa lifted her gaze to his, but she couldn't read his expression. His stoic face didn't indicate what he was thinking at all. Did he still want her in his life? Not just as a lover, but in her role as partner and mother of his children? If only she could see some softening in him, anything to give her a hint in which direction to go. If she only knew whether or not he wanted her to stay, or was telling her she was free to go his way of politely getting rid of her?

"Well, then," she said, forcing herself to sound upbeat and trying to act as if her heart weren't breaking. "That's good news." If she weren't careful, she would start blubbering like an idiot. *Remain calm.* "I could leave tonight." *Or never.*

"That won't be necessary, but of course, the choice is yours. We can move as quickly as you like."

He was still as cool as a cucumber. She was as hopeless in her efforts to read his expression as she was in reading Portuguese.

"I'll leave tonight."

There was no other choice. She couldn't stay in one of the guest rooms, pining away for him. She was worried she would find herself back in their suite, pleading with him to find a way to work things out. She couldn't remain here, in the room with him, because it would be too difficult, and if he touched her and made love to her again, it would make leaving in the morning even more difficult. Her only choice was to leave tonight so she could run back to her small condo and weep in private.

He didn't respond to her statement. Instead, he turned away from her and unzipped his jeans.

"I'm going for a swim."

It wasn't unusual for Leonardo to go for a swim in the nude because of the privacy afforded by the private courtyard. Nonetheless, it was jarring to watch the jeans lower down his bronze, muscular thighs and expose his taut buttocks. She took a mental photograph of his magnificent body as he exited the door, because she realized that would be the last time she ever saw him naked. Perhaps the last time she ever saw him, period.

That last thought was too much. The tears erupted out of her like an uncontrolled geyser, flooding her cheeks and seeping through the fingers covering her face. She sobbed for several minutes before finally rushing into the bathroom and locking the door. She couldn't risk him seeing her like this. It would be too humiliating.

Everything she'd been feeling over the past four months, and even the months before that, burst out. All her insecurities. All her feelings of neglect when he seemed to want to spend more time working than he did with her. All her fears of starting a family and not having him as a willing co-parent in the life of their children. She couldn't stop the tears. The dam had burst, and since she couldn't stem the flood of tears once they were unleashed, she leaned against the wall, sobbing until they stopped on their own.

THE MOTION LIGHTS on the ground floor shone their light onto the pool area. Leonardo's sinewy muscles glistened as he torpedoed through the water, doing his best to burn off the pain of Alexa's rejection. She couldn't have been clearer that she wanted out of their marriage. She became giddy at the prospect. To insist on leaving tonight was proof that no matter what had transpired between them over the past couple of days, she couldn't stand to be there a minute longer than was necessary.

He'd suspected what her answer would be. Yet, to watch her transform so immediately, it was a crushing blow. She couldn't wait to get away from him.

Levering himself out of the pool, Leonardo swept his wet hair back from his face.

It couldn't end like this. She had loved him once. He'd never heard her say the words, but he was sure of it. He could see it in the way her brown eyes used to light up when he approached. Surely they could work on their marriage and find something that was still worth salvaging.

Leonardo made it up the stairs in record time, but when he entered the bedroom, the familiar heavy quiet that was over the room made his heart beat faster than the laps he had swum.

"Alexa!" he called.

Like a madman, he pushed open the door to her closet. The lights were turned off. He looked over toward the bathroom. The door was cracked, and he could see the light was on in there. Maybe she hadn't heard him. He rushed over to the door, but he knew the truth before he pushed it open so hard it slammed against the wall with the force of a storm gale.

"Alexa!" Her name was torn from his throat and reverberated in the empty bathroom.

Two platinum rings jeered at him from the counter.

She was gone.

CHAPTER 9

$\mathcal{T}$he first few days after Alexa left, she'd secretly hoped
Leonardo would come after her. She clearly hadn't
learned her lesson from the first time. He didn't come. He didn't
call.

She didn't tell Xander right away that she and Leonardo
were no longer together. She couldn't face her brother, but he
soon found out what had taken place. The Monday after her
weekend with Leonardo, Xander showed up at the mansion
with a large cake and some smaller, specially made desserts.
Congratulations and Thank You the cake read, serving the dual
purpose of recognizing they were back together and showing
his appreciation for the money Leonardo had given him.

When he arrived at her doorstep forty-five minutes later, she
fell apart and let him comfort her as she sobbed out an explanation of how nothing had changed and she and Leonardo were
no longer going to be together. She carefully skated over
Xander's innocent role in the argument that ultimately forced
them apart again.

* * *

FIVE MONTHS after her second departure from the mansion, Alexa stood in the ballroom of the Royale Hotel in Atlanta. Tonight was a fundraiser for Second Chance Closet, and she had arrived early to ensure the final details were handled and everything went off without a hitch.

The huge room was still empty except for the local jazz band setting up onstage and the servers making last-minute touches to the room. The musicians were friends of her brother's, and Alexa appreciated the generosity of them volunteering their time and talent.

She felt the butterflies resurface in her stomach as she looked around for the event planner, Clarissa Beauchamp. Alexa had met and been impressed by Clarissa's efficiency when she'd attended a party at the hotel with Leonardo two years ago.

Just then, she saw the dark-skinned woman enter from a door near the back of the room. When she saw her, the tension she'd been harboring left her body.

Clarissa hurried over, wearing a pair of ballerina flats that Alexa knew she would exchange for pumps once the festivities were underway.

"Everything's fine," Clarissa said, giving Alexa a big smile and reassuring hug. She was petite and spoke in a soft, but firm tone, her Caribbean accent giving a melodic quality to her voice. She directed a smile over Alexa's shoulder to Xander, who had just walked in, looking handsome in a charcoal gray suit. Xander slipped his arm around his sister, and she leaned into him. "The food is ready, and the band's setting up," Clarissa continued.

The hotel had made an exception and allowed Xander's bakery to donate the dessert for the event. It hadn't been easy, but somehow Clarissa managed to convince them to do it. Alexa was very grateful because it not only cut down on costs, but it would give Xander's business exposure, as well.

"You've done such an exceptional job," Alexa said. "The room looks great."

Her eyes swept over the round tables of six. Each one held a small floral centerpiece and place cards for the invitees. There was a microphone and stand on the floor below the stage.

Grinning from ear to ear, Clarissa motioned with her hand and led Alexa and Xander to a table at the front.

"This is where you'll be seated with Edna and the volunteers from Second Chance Closet." Clarissa twisted her wrist to look at her watch again. "I'm going to the back to make sure we're still on schedule. If you need anything—anything at all—just tell one of the servers, and they'll find me, okay?"

"I will, but I'm not worried. I know I can be a bit anal, but I trust you, and I know the evening will go well."

"Well, you shouldn't be concerning yourself with trivialities anyway. You don't want all that negative energy going into the baby."

Alexa nodded her agreement. She slid her hand slowly over her five-months belly, which protruded just below the Empire waist of the black evening gown.

Two months after leaving Leonardo, she found out she was pregnant. It had been a shock because she was still on the Pill. However, her doctor reminded her the Pill was 99.9 percent effective when taken correctly, and she happened to fall into the very rare smaller percentage this time.

After Clarissa walked away, Alexa turned to Xander, who was now seated at the table, his ankle resting on his knee.

"Let Clarissa do her job," he said. "She's good at what she does, and that way you can relax."

"I will, but you know how I get. I can't help myself." She sat down next to him.

"How are you holding up?" Xander asked, concern in his soft brown eyes.

Alexa glanced away. Whenever he looked at her like that, she would get choked up. "I'm a grown woman. You should stop worrying about me."

"You're my sister. Just like you worry about me, I worry about you."

She reached for his hand on the table. "I'm healthy. My baby is healthy. My charity is successful. What more could I ask for?"

Xander shook his head, signifying his disapproval. "Come on, Lexie. This is me. You shouldn't do this on your own. It's not right, and it's not fair to Leo."

"I'm not doing it on my own." She withdrew from him. This conversation was a repeat of one they'd had several times since she found out about her pregnancy.

"Yes, you are!" He leaned forward. "You haven't even told him you're pregnant. I couldn't imagine what that would feel like to find out my wife was pregnant and she didn't tell me."

"Your relationship is different."

"How?"

"You two love each other. Leo and I . . . Leo doesn't love me." When he looked about to argue, she rushed on. "I know I have to tell him, and I will. I promise you, I won't keep it from him indefinitely."

"It'll hurt him when he finds out," Xander said reproachfully. She knew from past discussions he couldn't understand her hesitation.

Listening to him talk about how hurt Leonardo would be almost made Alexa smile. He made it sound as if Leonardo experienced the same emotions as the rest of the mere mortals. Little did he know, Leonardo didn't need anyone, and whatever he may feel when he found out she was pregnant, it wouldn't be hurt.

He might want to wring her neck, but he would refrain for the sake of the unborn child he'd tried in the past to convince her to carry. She knew she should tell him about the baby, but she was worried he would try to resume their marriage. That wasn't what she wanted—at least, not for that reason.

She wanted him to reach out to her because he loved her, not because she was having his child.

"I'll tell him when the time is right."

Xander looked skeptical. "The time was right three months ago when you found out for sure."

Alexa sighed and rested her hand on her stomach. "I know." This was the first instance since they were kids that Xander had been so displeased with her, and it made her unhappy.

She knew she should tell Leonardo. She just didn't have the guts to face him. Plus, she had been so busy with Second Chance Closet, the fundraiser, checkups, and morning sickness, that before she knew it, three months had passed and she hadn't contacted Leonardo.

Well, that wasn't entirely true. One day she did call, but his assistant stated he was out of the country and asked if someone else could help her. She'd wanted to leave the message, *It's his wife, and I'm pregnant.* But she didn't.

At some point she would have to tell him.

* * *

THE EVENING WAS A SMASHING SUCCESS. Of the over one hundred people in attendance, a number of them represented businesses. One company in particular, Demming Technology, a successful software company based in Atlanta, made a sizeable donation in addition to the funds they had paid for attending the event. This prompted others to do the same.

The total funds raised for Second Chance Closet were more than Alexa expected. Her mind was already racing as she envisioned what she could do with the money, such as opening a second store outside the city limits in Gwinnett or DeKalb County.

"Good night." Alexa waved to the last of her guests as they left. She was sitting at the table in front of the stage.

Xander sauntered over. "You did good," he said proudly. He dropped a gentle kiss on top of her curls.

"Thanks. I can't believe how much money we raised." The satchel containing all of the checks was on the table next to her laptop.

He nodded. "When it turns out better than you expected, that means you did a great job. And I made some good contacts tonight, so I expect business will increase for me in the near future."

"Yes. Just make sure you give Ryan all the contacts so he can follow up."

Ryan, who started out as a part-time office manager, had turned out to be invaluable. He was now the bakery's full-time operations manager and was in charge of business development. He was as indispensable to Xander's business as the commercial ovens.

"*I know.*" Xander rolled his eyes.

Fighting back a grin, Alexa glanced around the room. "Well, I'm going to—" She broke off when Xander's phone rang.

He answered, listened for a few seconds, and then said in a weary voice, "Yes, dear. I'm on my way home, and don't worry, I won't forget to stop at the store. I have the list with me." He rolled his eyes, pretending to be annoyed with his wife. After a few noncommittal words, he hung up. "All right, I need to leave," he said to Alexa. "I've been summoned. Let's get your stuff and get out of here."

Xander picked up her laptop and satchel, while Alexa eased her weary body out of the chair. It had been a long day. She was only five months along, but she was feeling the effects of her pregnancy—most notably in her lower back.

"Alexa."

The sound of her name caught her attention, but it was the

recognition of the person who spoke it that stilled her fingertips where she was absentmindedly massaging the base of her spine.

Gradually, she turned her body ninety degrees in the direction of her husband's voice. He stood a few feet from Xander, his expression giving away nothing.

He'd changed since the last time she saw him. His face looked bleak. Was it her imagination, or did he look thinner, too? The lines of his handsome face and the angles of his cheekbones appeared more pronounced.

"What are you doing here?"

"I heard about the fundraiser."

Xander spoke up. "Maybe I should go."

Alexa felt lost, panicked. She didn't want to be left alone with Leonardo. This was all so unexpected.

"We're about to leave," she said.

"We need to talk."

Xander chimed in. "That sounds like a good idea." Before Alexa could disagree, he put the satchel and laptop back on the table.

"What are you doing?" Alexa demanded frantically. Her eyes widened in dismay. Xander was abandoning her.

"He's right. You need to talk." He touched his lips to her temple. "Call me later."

As he was walking away, a look passed between him and Leonardo. She knew she didn't imagine it, and she figured she knew what had happened. Within seconds, she was left alone with her husband.

"You knew, didn't you?" She placed a hand on her stomach.

"Yes."

"How did you find out?"

"Xander."

Xander! Her own brother, just as she suspected. Where were his loyalties? Apparently they could be bought with a quarter of a million dollars. "When?"

"Two days ago. I was in Rio, and I flew back as quickly as I could." Quiet descended on the room. He was staring at her protruding belly as if he'd never seen a pregnant woman before. "Am I so horrible that you would keep my own child from me?"

Guilt assailed her, making her wish she had made more of an effort to contact him sooner. "I wasn't planning to exclude you from our child's life."

"Then why didn't you call me and let me know you were pregnant?" he asked, stark emotion etched in his face.

"I did, but when you weren't in, I . . . don't know. I needed time to think, to make a decision about what to do."

"A decision? There's no decision to be made. There's only one way this can go. Starting now, I want to be a part of my child's life. I intend to participate in everything, going to the doctor's visits, making sure you have the proper prenatal care, looking at the ultrasounds. I won't be excluded!" His voice became louder and harsher at the end. "I'm sorry," he said more calmly, running his fingers through his hair. Alexa noted they were shaking a bit. "I shouldn't upset you in your fragile state."

"I understand that you're angry." Alexa clasped her hands in front of her. "I should have told you."

His gaze flicked over her. "Are you well? Is everything fine with the baby?"

Alexa nodded. "I had a checkup a few days ago."

"Is it a boy or a girl?"

She shrugged. "I don't know. I didn't want to know. Not yet." *Not without you there, too.*

"Were you ever going to tell me?" he whispered.

She could see the pain in his eyes, and it grieved her that she had been the one to inflict it on this big, strong man. Xander had been right, and she had been wrong. He was hurt. Tears sprung to her eyes.

"Of course! I wouldn't keep you from your own child."

"It happens often enough nowadays, and it's not as if you

need me or anything I have to offer. Each time you left me, you left behind everything I ever gave you." He clenched his jaw, an indication he was crushing some deep emotion.

"I didn't need any of those things." She averted her eyes. "I swear to you, I would have told you. I know how much you wanted a child, and it would be wrong for me to keep you apart."

"I want you to come home, Alexa."

She looked into the bottomless depths of his black eyes. "No," she said firmly.

"Why not?" Leonardo demanded, his brow furrowing with displeasure. "I don't want to be cut off from my own child."

"You won't be cut off. You'll have as much access as you want, but I'm not moving back in with you." She swallowed hard, hating to tell him what she was about to say. "I've contacted an attorney. I want a divorce."

He looked shell-shocked, as if he couldn't fathom how she could say something so outrageous.

"You want to divorce me *now*?"

"It should have been done a long time ago. We're not happy together, and staying together for the sake of a child is not a good reason."

"I'm not giving you a divorce," he said evenly, struggling to remain calm. "You're pregnant with my child! I'm not letting you go."

"Why not?" Alexa asked, her voice wobbling. "You did before. Because I'm pregnant you want to hold on to me? I'm important to you now?" Alexa could feel the tears burning her eyes, and she willed herself not to cry. "I won't step foot back in that house, because nothing's changed."

"What is it that you want?" Leonardo asked, spreading his palms upward in exasperation. "You left me—twice. You chose to leave, and it didn't matter what I wanted. What is it that needs to change? Talk to me. Tell me what you want. We have to figure this out and make it work. I know what it did to my father when my mother and I moved away from him. I have to be there, every day, every night."

"Will you really be there?" she asked.

"Yes," he promised. "I've worked with an attorney at Russell's practice for the past year. She showed me how I could restructure the firm and still maintain the level of control I'd be comfortable with even though the day-to-day operations would be handled by my top executives."

Alexa knew it was difficult for him to release control. "I can't believe you did that."

"Believe it." He stepped closer. "I *will* be there, Alexa. I won't neglect my child. Is that all you want?"

Alexa felt her face crumble. She should be stronger than this. It was a simple question, but her doctor had warned her she could become emotional since her hormones were out of whack. That had to be the reason why the tears burned past her throat and fell onto her cheeks unrestrainedly.

She bit her lip and brushed them away, but others quickly replaced them.

"Alexa," Leonardo groaned. He reached for her, then thought better of it and pulled back.

"*Maldição.*" The soft curse seemed torn from him. "What is it?"

"Hormones," she said brokenly.

"No. Tell me, what is it that you want?"

She couldn't reveal what she secretly yearned for. It was foolish to spill everything inside her heart. Because even though it was clear Leonardo wanted and already loved their unborn child, it was equally plain he didn't love her. She'd been gone five months, and the only reason he was standing in front of her was because he found out she was pregnant.

"I have to go." She turned back to the table to pick up her belongings. "We can talk later."

"We will talk now. We never talk." He took her gently, but firmly by the arm and turned her back to face him. "What do you want, Alexa?"

She pulled back, but his gentleness was her undoing. "I want you to love me." She couldn't retract the words, and even though he looked stunned, confused, it was a relief to tell him how she truly felt. "You've never said it. I've never heard you say you love me, Leo."

"I didn't think I needed to. I thought giving you everything you wanted was proof of my love for you. I worked hard to provide for you."

"You've always worked hard, and you know I don't care about those *things*," Alexa said.

His expression became bleaker. "I know . . . and yet . . ." He shook his head as his words trailed off. "I can't let you go, Alexa."

"You already did," she whispered. "You only came back because you found out I was pregnant, and I won't subject my child to the life my brother and I had to endure as children. I won't fight with you all the time in front of our child, and I won't let you ignore our child so you can spend all your time at work. I already know what it feels like, and I won't do that to my baby." She spread protective fingers across her stomach.

Leonardo's gaze followed the gesture. "Your pregnancy isn't the only reason I returned. It just caused me to return sooner." He lifted his eyes to her face. "My work is important to me, but you're more important. When I moved to Rio three months ago, I wanted nothing more than to take you with me, but I realized I would be subjecting you to the same treatment as before. I had to spend the time necessary to launch our Latin American head-quarters.

"Before our first separation, I was working like a man who wasn't married, and that wasn't fair to you. It's all I know, *querida*. It's what I saw my father do all his life. I was five when my parents divorced, so I didn't fully understand why my mother left."

He stepped closer to her. "I've spoken to my mother, and I understand now. I've changed. I don't work the same hours, and I've been making preparations for you to come live with me. Everything isn't ready, but I had to come get you as soon as I found out about your pregnancy. I'm not giving you a divorce, and I'm not leaving without you."

Leonardo took her face in his hands and looked down into her water-filled eyes. *"Meu amor,"* he murmured, pressing his lips against her cheeks to kiss away her tears. "How could you doubt how much I love you, when I can't even sleep without you beside me?"

Alexa's eyes widened in her face.

"Eu te amo, querida," he whispered. "I love you so much, that if you don't come back to stay, I think I'll die this time."

Alexa couldn't believe it. Finally, the words she longed to hear were released from the lips of the only man she'd ever loved. Getting up on tiptoe, she flung her arms around his neck. "I've waited so long to hear you say that."

"I'll say it every day for the rest of our lives." Leonardo rained little kisses across her eyelids, down her nose, and across each cheek, warming her insides. *"Eu te amo. Eu te amo. Eu te amo."*

Alexa looked up into the eyes of her husband. She believed him. He'd changed, and she would, too. She had been afraid of turning into her mother. She had been worried her marriage would mirror the unhappy mess her parents' had been.

She would no longer hide her feelings, and she would let Leonardo know if she felt neglected. She couldn't expect him to know what was wrong if she wasn't vocal about her needs.

She pulled down his head and pressed her lips against his. "I love you, too."

EPILOGUE

*A*lexa's bare feet padded softly across the tile covering the rooftop patio where Leonardo was reclining, the cell phone glued to his ear as he conducted business in Portuguese. The sun was low in the sky, but it was still warm in Rio de Janeiro, where they'd been living for the past year.

Their daughter, Lucélia, was born in Brazil, where Leonardo was successfully spearheading the launch of Radiant Communications into the Latin American market. In a couple of years, they planned to return to the United States once the business was established.

As Radiant Communications flourished, so did Second Chance Closet. There was now a smaller store in DeKalb County, and the larger one in Atlanta had grown by taking over empty retail space next to it. Additional staff was hired and more volunteers recruited to help Edna, who became the general manager and oversaw the running of both stores. She and Alexa held weekly meetings via Skype and communicated via e-mail.

Alexa set a glass of *caipirinha* on the table next to Leo. She was proud that she had become an expert at fixing Brazil's national drink just the way Leonardo liked it. However, she was unable to indulge herself at this time, settling for a glass of the Brazilian soda *guaraná*, since they'd gotten the good news just days before that she was pregnant again.

Alexa cleared her throat loudly, settling a hand on her hip. It was a few minutes after seven. Business was cutting into her time.

Leonardo's appreciative gaze ran over her shapely figure in the sarong and bikini top. Smiling, he spoke rapidly, then hung up with a brisk *"Ciao."*

"Come here," he said, setting her glass next to his on the table.

Gladly, Alexa sat on his lap, draping her arms around his neck.

"Where is Lucélia?" he asked.

"Downstairs with your mother, taking a nap."

"Hmm . . . interesting." He ran his warm palm down her back. Her body's instantaneous reaction was to heat up. "Have I told you I love you today?"

"No, you haven't," Alexa said saucily, cocking her ear toward him.

"Eu te amo, meu amor," he whispered hotly. He then plucked at the fleshy lobe of her ear with his lips.

"Leo, behave," she said halfheartedly as heat began to pool between her legs.

"I can't," he said, nuzzling her neck. "Your brother and his family will be here tomorrow, and they're staying for a couple of weeks. Including my mother, that's three other adults and a total of five children. I have a feeling our sex life won't be the same for a while, so I'm getting all I can now."

"In that case . . ." Alexa stood up. His pupils dilated when he saw her reach behind her back and undo her top. "Come get me."

She tossed the bikini in his face, but before she could get away, he was already on his feet. He swept her up in his arms to her squeals of delight.

"I always do."

Then Leonardo strode into the house with Alexa in his arms.

ALSO BY DELANEY DIAMOND

Check out the entire Latin Men series with heroes from Mexico, Ecuador, Brazil, and Argentina: The Arrangement, Fight for Love, Private Acts, The Ultimate Merger, Second Chances, More Than a Mistress, and Undeniable.

ABOUT THE AUTHOR

Delaney Diamond is the USA Today Bestselling Author of sweet, sensual, passionate romance novels. Originally from the U.S. Virgin Islands, she now lives in Atlanta, Georgia. She reads romance novels, mysteries, thrillers, and a fair amount of nonfiction. When she's not busy reading or writing, she's in the kitchen trying out new recipes, dining at one of her favorite restaurants, or traveling to an interesting locale.

Enjoy free reads on her website. Join her mailing list to get sneak peeks, notices of sale prices, and find out about new releases.

Join her mailing list
www.delaneydiamond.com

f facebook.com/DelaneyDiamond
🐦 twitter.com/DelaneyDiamond
BB bookbub.com/authors/delaney-diamond
P pinterest.com/delaneydiamond

Printed in Great Britain
by Amazon